MW00944437

DON'T BLAME THE MESSENGER

Lee Kronert

WESTBOW
PRESS

A DIVISION OF THOMAS NELSON

Copyright © 2012 Lee Kronert

All rights reserved. No part of this book may be used or reproduced by any means, graphic, electronic, or mechanical, including photocopying, recording, taping or by any information storage retrieval system without the written permission of the publisher except in the case of brief quotations embodied in critical articles and reviews.

WestBow Press books may be ordered through booksellers or by contacting:

WestBow Press
A Division of Thomas Nelson
1663 Liberty Drive
Bloomington, IN 47403
www.westbowpress.com
1-(866) 928-1240

Because of the dynamic nature of the Internet, any web addresses or links contained in this book may have changed since publication and may no longer be valid. The views expressed in this work are solely those of the author and do not necessarily reflect the views of the publisher, and the publisher hereby disclaims any responsibility for them.

Any people depicted in stock imagery provided by Thinkstock are models, and such images are being used for illustrative purposes only.

Certain stock imagery © Thinkstock.

ISBN: 978-1-4497-6784-6 (sc)
ISBN: 978-1-4497-6785-3 (hc)
ISBN: 978-1-4497-6783-9 (e)

Library of Congress Control Number: 2012917251

Printed in the United States of America

WestBow Press rev. date: 11/8/2012

Edited by Amanda Kronert

To Joe Blanda: Who taught me how to write and inspired me to join the ranks of one of the greatest professions on earth: A School Teacher!

Introduction

The New York State Commissioner of Education, Robert Haines, smiled at the President of the New York State Teachers' Association, Linda Malachi.

"Don't be ridiculous," he chided the newly elected leader. "I am not trying to eliminate tenure."

"Then why," Ms. Malachi sneered, "are these new teacher evaluations even being introduced?"

Robert Haines stared at the woman. He was in no mood to face or answer to any her annoying accusations. Haines only granted the NEA President a meeting because he'd already canceled or avoided several others.

"The updated Annual Performance Plan Reviews," he dryly continued, "are being put into effect, because the public is demanding a change in education. Parents are tired of dealing with incompetent teachers and want better prepared instructors for their children. We are both parents. I'm sure that like me, you want a quality education for your kids. What parent doesn't?

"These updated guidelines will help weed out those teachers who perhaps should be dedicating themselves to a different field. There are currently so many young, capable, and energetic college graduates who cannot find jobs in our public schools. I dare say a good number of these young people are more qualified than some of the existing teachers in our system. We have too many older teachers who lack the ability to effectively connect with the modern student. It's a big problem Linda, and the time has come to do something about it."

"So you want to fire the experienced teachers?"

"I didn't say that. We're not looking to fire anybody! All the state of New York is trying to do is create ways to determine who the best teachers are and reward them accordingly."

"And fire the rest!"

Linda Malachi had heard this type of rhetoric before. These new updated Annual Performance Plan Reviews (APPR) were, in her opinion, merely a new means to undermine a teacher's right to tenure. Once a public school teacher worked at their job for three years, it was now impossible to get rid of them. They were now tenured. It was like the three years were a probationary figure that once reached, established a teacher forever in their particular school district. Simply put, tenure meant that a teacher had lifetime job security. It was true that not all teachers were great at teaching. She could easily think of many individuals that she would love to see on another career path, but eliminating tenure would be going too far. It would mean that any teacher could lose their job at any time and for any souped-up reason. Although the system of tenure had its faults, it seemed to be the best way to ensure that schools didn't lose a whole bunch of good teachers along with the bad ones.

Linda Malachi held up the new and recently approved state manual for teacher evaluations. "It says here, on page five, that the main indicator of proficiency in a teacher would be his or her classes' results on the state exams. Are you kidding me?"

"According to the No Child Left Behind Act, every kid in school should be taught well enough to be successful." Haines interrupted. "There are not supposed to be any failures. But unfortunately, we've got kids failing and dropping out all over the place. Teachers need to be held accountable. These new teacher evaluations are a way of making sure we have the best teachers in order to meet the No Child Left Behind goals."

"I used to be in the classroom," she explained. "I taught for many years, and many of my students failed to do their homework or had either their heads down or backs turned during my instruction. I know that you would never mean to insinuate that *I* am unfit to teach. How can any teacher be held responsible for poor scores when faced with the rude and obnoxious behavior that is present in many classrooms, particularly in districts that are struggling economically? As far as I'm concerned, this new teacher evaluation form is sabotage. There's nothing fair about it."

Linda Malachi may have been newly elected, but she was not afraid to confront the leadership in Albany. Her feisty attitude had actually swayed many of the voters who had won her the position. Malachi was the Union's perfect choice for leadership. While the State Education Department was idealistic and held a negative view of teachers and the present condition of education, Linda Malachi was not only a former teacher who saw the positive aspects of today's educators, but a leader who was realistic about the students, teachers, and administrators who were trying to right the public education ship. These were tough times in the field of education, and a person willing to fight for the rights of teachers was sorely needed.

The leadership in Albany was frustrated by her election as President of the state-wide teachers' association. Commissioner of Education, Robert Haines, had already met with the little spitfire a few times too many, and while he was impressed with her knowledge and tenacity, he found her manner irksome and unbecoming, particularly in a woman.

"The same exam is tendered throughout the entire state of New York," Haines defended. "That means that the tests are fair. Whether you are wealthy, poor, wear the best clothes, or are on free or reduced lunch, every kid takes the same test. There are no socio-economic advantages nor is there any cultural favoritism. The tests are the same for everybody. If some school districts fail to measure up, than there are clearly issues that need to be addressed."

Linda Malachi's face spoke before her mouth could spit the words. "Are you serious?" she screamed. "Are you going to sit there and tell me that the kids from the inner city are on equal footing with the kids from the Hamptons?"

"No, I'm not." Haines hissed back. "My guess is that the Hamptons employ the cream of the crop. Those teachers who cannot secure positions in the suburbs probably wind up in the city where the school districts are desperate for all the help they can get!"

"Did I just hear you say what I thought I heard you say?"

The Commissioner did not reply. Instead, he simply sat still and spread out his arms. The pompous gesture said it all.

"You and Albany are going to blame the teachers for the low scores in New York City, Buffalo, Rochester, and Syracuse? Really? You're suggesting that a child, who has grown up in a crack house, or a child who becomes pregnant at thirteen, cannot pass his or her state exam because his or her *teacher* is not doing his or her job?"

The phone on the Commissioner's desk rang. Haines quickly seized the phone, desperate to be involved with anything other than this annoying woman.

"Yes?"

Robert Haines raised his eyebrows in an expression of concern, as he listened to the voice rattle on the other end of the line. Linda Malachi studied his face and quickly concluded, *the jerk is acting like he's listening to something terribly important, and he's acting it out for my sake.*

She was right.

"Of course, I will be right there."

When the Commissioner hung up the phone, he immediately cleared his throat, "I am so sorry for the interruption, but I am afraid I have an important matter to deal with downtown. It just won't wait."

He stood up and stretched out his hand. "It was good to see you again, Linda," he lied. "Perhaps we can consider resuming our conversation at a later date."

He swiftly escorted the indignant woman to the door of his office and out into the hallway. When he saw that Linda was about to turn left, he made a quick turn to the right and briskly made his way towards the elevators. As he pounded the down arrow, he glanced furtively over his shoulder. Linda Malachi was out of sight. Mission accomplished!

How clever! The phone call was from his daughter Annie, inviting him out to lunch. A junior at Albany University, Annie was always extending invitations for lunches, lectures, and concerts, which he was usually too busy to attend. Under normal circumstances, he would have made an excuse not to meet, but today her offer was the perfect escape.

He gave his little girl a big hug at the entrance to their favorite restaurant. The waitress gestured to a small booth towards the back and they sat down on opposite sides of the table. He had to admit, he felt a little guilty as he sat admiring his beautiful daughter. Tall, thin, and dark, she looked just like her Daddy, sharing even his mesmerizing blue eyes. She was smart like him also. She always had been at the very top of her class. *I should be here for her more often.*

"I think I've decided," she announced.

He and Annie had discussed the selection of her major several times in the past three years and yet, so far she had shown no inclination that she was ready to decide anything! But something was different today. Her bright blue eyes were beaming, and Robert Haines saw the passion and determination he so admired in himself staring right back at him.

"I want to be a school teacher!"

Chapter 1

His alarm went off at six o'clock in the morning. Brendan Moss was ready. It was the Tuesday morning following Labor Day. Summer vacation was over and another year of school was about to begin. Brendan always joked that his two favorite words in the English language were July and August, but when the early days of September arrived he was ready to return to his vocation, or as he liked to put it, his calling!

As was his usual routine, Brendan had shaved and showered the night before. That way, the next morning he could just climb out of bed, wash his face and teeth, and dress before leaving the house promptly at 6:15.

He quickly ate some breakfast while filling his duffel bag. Once the bag was packed, he hoisted it over his shoulder and caught his reflection in the mirror by the door. A relatively short man at 5'7", with a bald head and sharp nose, Brendan had developed a little pouch over the years, but otherwise his looks belied his sixty years. *Not too bad*, he thought.

On the thirty-five minute drive to Riverton Middle School, Brendan continued his morning routine with silent prayer. He would ask God to protect and bless his three children, and would ask nothing more for himself. His two sons, Jonathan and Matthew, still lived with him in his home in Ashton, New York, while his eldest daughter Amanda now lived with her husband Brian in Syracuse, New York. He missed his daughter, but he had known that this time would come, and to some degree was prepared for the day he had had to give his daughter away. Nothing, however could have prepared him for the loss of Emily. Your wife was not supposed to die at forty-five.

Even now, close to five years later, Brendan still missed the love of his life terribly. They were soul mates, best friends, and ardent lovers. They were supposed to be together forever!

He had cried three weeks ago at Amanda's wedding. The ceremony had been so beautiful, and his baby girl had looked so joyous on her special day. It had made him think about his own wedding day, and he was painfully reminded that his own bride no longer stood beside him.

Brendan Moss did his best to continue being a good father to all three of his children. Although Amanda was now married, Matt was attending the local junior college, and Jonathan, a senior in high school, was beginning his final varsity season in soccer. In addition to being a single father at home, Brendan continued his work as an eighth grade math teacher in Riverton, New York.

Brendan normally arrived at Riverton Middle School around 6:50 in the morning. Although he was not required to be there until 7:20, he came in earlier to write. A newly published author, Brendan Moss was just now finishing up his third novel. Writing was a way of clearing his head. It was, as he often told others, his choice of therapy.

It was September the fifth, and there wouldn't be any students in the middle school. Brendan's official first day of work was a Superintendent's Day, where all of the staff at Riverton would be welcomed back and updated on the administration's goals for the year. As always, the majority of the agenda focused on the latest decisions by the State Department of Education.

The Riverton Superintendent, Bailey Thompson, tapped the microphone to let the staff know that things were about to begin. It was Mr. Thompson's first day on the job. Formally a principal in Tonawanda, New York, the newly hired superintendent was anxious and eager to introduce himself to the Riverton staff.

"Good morning everyone," he welcomed. "I hope you are as excited as I am to start a new school year."

Brendan had attended almost thirty of these presentations and usually found them boring. As usual, he chose a seat some distance away from his coworkers so that he could read a chapter in his Bible and work on his novel during the orientation. He soon found that these distractions were unnecessary. Thompson was a humorous and entertaining speaker. He presented his ideas both clearly and logically and further appealed to the audience's interests by sharing stories, offering analogies, and adding humorous antidotes. *This guy probably used to be a teacher!*

After finishing a funny tale about his car troubles, Bailey Thompson grew more serious. "Now there are of course, going to be some changes that need to be implemented."

Uh-oh. Enter the powers that be from the State of New York.

"Our test scores," the superintendent grimaced, "are among the lowest in Western New York, and they have been for several years now. This trend cannot continue. There needs to be a change."

We need to change. We need to do things differently. We need to raise our test scores. We! We! We! Everybody knew what that meant. The teachers at Riverton had better figure out how to get their act together. We were the problem. Did it ever occur to anyone in administration or Albany that the problem just might be the kids we teach?

"In English and math," the superintendent continued, "the state would like each teacher to create tests every eight weeks to assess mastery. The tests must be reviewed and approved by the building principal and graded by the teachers. Albany has asked that each of these eight week tests be patterned after the actual state exams."

A hand was raised. Bailey Thompson acknowledged it.

"The state won't let us keep the exams, so how can we pattern our tests after an exam that we're not allowed to see?"

Chuckles rippled throughout the auditorium.

Thompson simply shrugged his shoulders and smiled.

That too caught Brendan's attention. *This guy knows. He understands that Albany is clueless.* It was a refreshing realization.

In the afternoon, all of the middle school teachers gathered in the library where the principal, Tyler Haden, prepared to address his staff. Once again, Brendan sat alone near the back. He just liked it that way.

Haden was a tall man, 6'3". Brendan and Tyler had been friends for years. Their friendship began when the two of them were both still teaching math at the high school. Brendan considered Tyler an excellent administrator and found that everyone on the staff shared his high opinion of the man. Here was a man who could be trusted to protect the people he worked with. Even though Haden was six years younger than him, Brendan looked up to Tyler. Not just because Tyler was tall!

The principal of Riverton Middle School introduced the new members of the staff, briefly out lined new disciplinary procedures, and shared some general information about the student's first day tomorrow. He then moved to the topic of teacher evaluations. The APPR, or Annual Performance Plan Review, had already been around for a few years by now. It was simply used as an indicator to assess how a teacher was progressing professionally. Brendan thought the whole concept was ridiculous, but he had dutifully filled in his form each year and had later presented evidence that his personal professional goals had been reached. *What was the point? No one really knew.*

In the early stages of the development of the APPR, the process had seemed relatively harmless. Teachers had agreed to stress certain areas of instruction, increase their use of technology, or demonstrate how they had utilized a reward system for students who had performed up to standards. Throughout the state, principals had whisked their staff in and out of their offices to dissect and discuss the ways that these goals could be met. A goal could be as simple as an attempt to show improvement in content areas through pre and post testing. Some teachers' APPRs had included a histogram designed to demonstrate increased proficiency in technology. It had seemed simple, even at times helpful, but through the years Brendan Moss had developed a theory. *Albany had a plan!*

"I would appreciate everyone getting their APPRs to me as quickly as possible," Principal Haden requested. "The sooner we get working on these things the better. That way I don't get all cluttered up next month trying to catch up."

The entire staff at Riverton Middle School loved Tyler Haden. He was fair. He had a good heart and a caring ear. His simple request was well received.

"The state," Tyler Haden continued, "has ordered that this year's APPR be more closely related to the state exam. The state requests that every English and math teacher list his or her areas of weakness and that he or she designate these areas as focus points."

A hand was raised. It belonged to Maya Gregg, the eighth grade English teacher. Maya was highly respected in the district, and despite the low scores on last year's test, she had not yet been confronted or chastised. Administration, for some reason, was afraid of Maya Gregg. No one had the guts to blame her for the test results.

"You said," Ms. Gregg evenly pronounced, "that each math and English teacher would need to address an area of weakness." She paused for effect. "Who's got the weakness: the teacher or the students?"

That, in a nutshell, was the big issue in education across the country. Who's to blame for the low scores and the increases in drop-out rate, criminal behavior, and bullying? The teachers or the students? It was a good question.

Brendan Moss shook his head. He liked Ms. Gregg's question. In fact, he kind of wished he'd asked the question first. He thought he knew how Albany would answer that question. Albany, he believed, would claim that many of today's teachers were unqualified to reach today's children. Albany would say that the state wide test scores fairly identified which school districts were failing. Further, he judged that they believed that the classrooms full of struggling students were being taught by inept teachers who had been granted tenure and who no one could get rid of.

How did Albany know that the teachers were lousy? The low test scores proved it! Did the state consider that low scores might be a result of poor attendance, learning disabilities, or apathy? Brendan thought not! The teacher, Albany would say, is responsible to motivate, stir participation, and make sure that each and every student demonstrates competency.

"I believe," Tyler Haden reiterated, "that an area of weakness refers solely to the material or information that a majority of students are failing to fully understand." Mr. Haden looked down at the sheet that he held in his hand, "Like say in math, the kids are having difficulty with transformations."

That statement caught Brendan Moss' attention. He had spent a few weeks last year on the topic of transformations. Transformations were drawings on a graph of such things as triangles, or squares, or other figures that a student would need to identify a particular movement of. The figure might translate to a different position on the graph or it might rotate or grow in size. Students were expected to identify and connect a math term to each type of change. He was quite familiar with the state standards, and he knew the types of questions normally asked about transformations. However on last spring's test, the state slightly altered the transformation problem and the minor change confused a large majority of the kids. The ambiguity of the question bordered on the ridiculous, and that one question was the only question asked on the topic of transformations. The state unjustly determined that Riverton Middle School had a weakness in the area of transformations, due to the large quantity of students who failed to correctly answer the question.

"Look," the middle school principal attempted to clarify, "I'm not the state, guys. I know how it might sound, but as long as I'm principal here in Riverton, no one is going to be blamed for low test scores."

Brendan believed him. Haden was a good man and a former teacher himself. He was well aware of the difficulty of motivating students in this town. He knew that his staff was not to blame.

Following the faculty meeting there was a brief meeting of the Riverton Teacher's Association (RTA) in the auditorium. No administrators were allowed.

The president of the RTA was a young, energetic fellow named Dan Ross. Ross taught high school science, and this year was the start of his first term as president of the association. He was thirty years old, short, but with a muscular build, and coached the boys' varsity wrestling team. Handsome and assertive, he was a good face for the organization, although Brendan found him to be a little too ambitious.

"Albany is out to get us," Dan Ross boldly claimed. "There is already an effort underway to remove our right to collective bargaining here in New York." Collective bargaining was the right of unions to demand owners of businesses to ensure safe working conditions, fair pay, and protection of their workers in any type of disputes. In education, the business owner was the State Education Department. And one of the major bargaining chips of the teacher's union was the concept of tenure. A tenured teacher could not lose their job unless they really did something stupid, dangerous to youth, or illegal. All of the teachers were well aware of a similar decision in Wisconsin to do away with the union's right to collective bargaining that had passed over the summer. It wasn't a surprise that New York would try to follow suit. "If ever there was a time to be careful, this is it, and I am referring to all areas of our profession." Ross coughed nervously. "Make sure that your APPRs are written to reflect areas of state testing, and be very certain to phrase your goals in a way in which you know they can be met."

Many heads in the audience nodded. People understood.

"Now we need to talk about discipline."

Riverton Middle School was nestled in a poor town among the hills of Western New York. Many of Riverton's inhabitants were unemployed, but could find good jobs if they wanted. A large majority of the population had small incomes simply because they didn't want to work! When Brendan and his wife Emily had originally moved to Western New York from New Jersey over twenty years ago, Riverton was a nice town, filled with lots of hospitality and buzzing with shops and activities. Things had changed. No one understood just how, but during the past ten years especially, an influx of welfare types moved in. With them came an increase in crime, soup kitchens, pawn shops, and new students who didn't seem to know the first thing about respect, loyalty, or honor.

How does one explain it? What exactly do rampant disrespect and welfare have in common? Brendan Moss never could quite figure it out.

His own father had grown up poor in Newark, New Jersey. His father was forced to quit school in the middle of the eighth grade, because he needed the money to help provide for his family. The less fortunate children in Riverton were never lacking material goods, unlike the children like his father in the nineteen-thirties.

How does one explain the lack of respect for authority figures in the school? Brendan knew poverty was not the only answer. Brendan's dad had worked hard his entire life and his father had built a good life for his family.

Will today's youth follow that blueprint? Brendan doubted it.

Now into his thirtieth year of teaching, Brendan strongly felt that he had an idea of where the problem lay. He'd seen it all in his thirty years. In each and every classroom the disparities stood side by side: the respectful and disrespectful, the kind and the mean, the diligent and the lazy, the positive and the negative attitudes, the committed and the selfish. There was no formula that explained all of the disparities, but there was certainly a familiar trend: the parents!

Okay, he did exaggerate. The reality was this: A vast majority of parents did want a good, solid education for their child, and they knew that if their child is not meeting set standards, that it is the child who is to blame and not the teacher.

Some parents however, did not blame their children when their children failed, but rather thought of their child's teacher as a villain. To some, teachers were "know it all's", looking down their noses at children who did not comply to their lofty standards. To such guardians, discipline was not an act of love, but a display of domination.

Who was right? Did the educational system need to weed out the bad teachers? Or did more parents need to discipline their children before a teacher was forced to?

"We have been designated as a dangerous school," Dan Ross proclaimed, with just a hint of remorse. "Albany has come out with a new school evaluation system. The new system tallies discipline reports, after school detentions, and in-and-out of school suspensions. This data is then compared with other districts of similar size and economic status. Riverton's reports are the worst in the county. Over the summer I attended meetings with the new superintendent and the other buildings' principals, and here's the deal. Administration is going to demand that we cut down on the number of discipline reports. They would like the teachers to address the majority of behavioral issues right in the classroom. Unless the situation is potentially dangerous, administration will no longer accept or act upon a written report. There's going to be a lot of wrist-slapping guys. If a child tells you to 'f-off', you will be expected to calm him down and take your own corrective measures. Administration only wants to deal with the big stuff."

"Which is what?" a voice cried out.

Ross shook his head derisively, "Murder and rape, I suppose."

That comment spurred a round of laughter. Ross waited for the chuckling to subside. "At the summer meetings, I took some notes on the types of misbehaviors principals do not wish to hear about. Here it goes," Ross began, lifting a clipboard from the podium. "Foul language, throwing objects, insubordination, bullying, bringing drugs to school as long as there is no attempt to sell, running in the hallways, pushing and shoving as long as no serious injury occurs, thefts under $100, and of course, failure to complete homework or pay attention during lectures."

"So the kids can do anything they want?" a different voice from the crowd called out.

"What is the point of this?" a third, concerned member of the Riverton district cried out.

"They want the teachers to handle the discipline in their classroom. If we can, as a school district, show a dramatic decrease in the volume of our disciplinary reports, then the dangerous label will be dropped. If not, and if we continue to be classified as a dangerous school, we could lose state funding. We would be placed on probation. People could lose their jobs."

Brendan Moss had heard enough. He rose to his feet. "I don't know about the rest of you, but I will not compromise my principles, just because a bunch of people up in Albany are clueless! When I was in the first grade there was a group of boys who teased me, pushed me around, and even spit on me at school. When I told my parents about it they were outraged. Oh, not because of the bullying itself, but because I didn't fight back! My father told me that I'd better do something about it. I was only six at the time, but I can still remember my Dad telling me, 'If you let them keep bullying you, it will never stop. You got to draw a line in the sand, and let them know that enough is enough.'"

Brendan cleared his throat.

"Albany and the State Ed Department are bullying us. They're calling us names and blaming the teachers for drop-out rates and the increase of crime in our schools. I am going to echo the words of my Dad. Enough is enough! They demand that we take a more proactive approach to discipline, but we can't touch them and we are told not to yell at them. Now they are ordering us to stop writing them up? This should show anyone who is paying attention that Albany is not on our side! They expect a rise in test scores while crippling our ability to discipline. I don't know about the rest of you, but I need classroom management to teach. We are a dangerous school, and we need the support from the state to do something about it!"

A loud burst of applause and whistles erupted from the crowd. Moss wasn't looking to be appreciated, but it was nice to know that his coworkers shared his views.

An hour later, as he was strolling down the hallway, he passed the president of the Riverton Teacher's Association. They greeted each other with a smile. "Mr. Moss, that was quite a little speech you gave today," said Dan Ross. "Everybody knows you're right," he affirmed, "including Albany."

"That's the scary part," Brendan responded.

"I know," Ross agreed. "That's what I'm worried about."

As Dan Ross watched the math teacher walk away, he was once again filled with a jealousy which he could not deny. He did not like Brendan Moss. Oh, it wasn't like Moss' character bothered him or anything like that. It was something else about the man. Ross recalled a couple of conversations he had had with the guy over the years.

Ross once overheard Moss make a statement which challenged the theory of evolution.

"I believe we've been on this earth for 6,000 years." Moss said as though it were fact.

Ross was a science teacher who totally embraced the theory of evolution. Moss' claim, that man has only been on earth for 6,000 years, was a personal affront to his professional sensibilities. It bothered him that the guy had the nerve to be such an open creationist theory proponent.

"Why do you believe such nonsense?" Dan Ross confronted Moss after a faculty meeting. "Science has facts and evidence which points to a world that has been here for millions of years."

Moss shrugged his shoulders and stated matter-of-factly, "I believe the Bible, Dan. That's all. If God says that we've only been here on earth for 6,000 years then I believe it."

As he now watched Moss walk away on this first day of a new school year Dan Ross comforted himself with a belief of his own.

'I'm the leader now, Mr. Moss. We'll see whom our staff listens to for inspiration, you or me!"

Chapter 2

Charles Hayes enjoyed school. He loved learning facts and handing in projects, and he relished classroom discussions. Math was his favorite subject. Today, September sixth, was his first day as a high school student, and he was well aware of just how hazardous the first day of high school might be.

At least he knew how to run! About the only thing Charles Hayes liked more than school was running, probably because he was so fast.

Splat! Something hit him on the side of his face. Whatever it was, it felt wet and slimy, and Charles instantly detected a putrid smell. As he turned around, wiping his face clean, he found he was surrounded by a few larger boys wearing football jerseys.

Well, nowhere to run, he supposed.

"Hey rookie," one of the boys taunted him, "welcome to Riverton High School."

"Uh, the middle school and high school are connected. I've eaten in the same cafeteria as you for the past three years," Charles couldn't help but point out.

Splat! This time a piece of cow liver struck the back of his head. Charles did a quick count before looking back at Buster McHale, the boy who had called him rookie.

"Really?" He directed at Buster. "Seven against one? How pathetic is that?"

Buster McHale made a fist and rushed towards Charles. Charles raised his arms over his head to block the blow, but the hit never came. Buster was torn away by a strong hand on the back of his shoulder. Charles peeked through the cracks in his fingers to see who had prevented the assault.

The hand belonged to Mr. Moss.

"Any problems, guys?" Brendan Moss asked the group.

"Hi, Mr. Moss!" Charles Hayes spoke excitedly. He was glad to see his favorite teacher, Mr. Moss. He hadn't seen his eighth grade math teacher since before the summer, and he was especially glad to see him now! His mood brightened instantly, and he nearly forgot that he was standing in the valley of death, surrounded by football players who wanted to hurt him!

"Hi Charles," Brendan answered back. "The bell's going to ring soon," he announced to the pack. "So let's get going boys."

Buster McHale glared at Mr. Moss. They had had issues in the past. As Buster passed past Charles, he purposely bumped his shoulder into the freshman. Mr. Moss took a step forward until he remembered: *No discipline reports allowed!*

"Thanks, Mr. Moss. I guess things could have gotten pretty messy back there," The kid smiled.

Brendan returned the smile. "I expect you to make me proud over at the high school," his former math teacher encouraged. "You were probably the best eighth grade math student I've ever had."

"Probably?"

That was what Brendan Moss liked so much about this kid. He was short and skinny, with flaming red curly hair and freckles too, but man, was the kid spunky! Rude, obnoxious boys like Buster McHale and his gang of terrorists picked on kids like Charles constantly. They made fun of his looks, his frailty, and the way he talked. The bullies even had the nerve to harass poor Charles because he excelled academically.

After observing Charles Hayes for the past two years, Brendan had come to this conclusion: *This kid is never going to back down! No matter how awful they treated him or how unfairly abused, Charles would always spring back with a mocking rebuttal. It was his way of saying, 'look at who the losers really are'.*

"All right," Brendan had to admit, "You are the best, smartest, funniest, and most awesome kid I've ever had the pleasure to teach."

This time the usually wise-cracking Charles had no comeback. He liked what he just heard.

"You're the best teacher I've ever had. When my parents split up, I was really lost, Mr. Moss. I've only seen my Dad twice in the last three years. So," he fumbled, "I always thought of you as kind of my substitute Dad. Every time the other boys tried to tease me or embarrass me, you seemed to be there to protect me, just like you did today."

For a second Brendan was speechless.

"I'd be very proud to have a son like you," the math teacher pronounced evenly. "You're going to be a huge success someday, Charlie Hayes, and I will be the first in line to congratulate you. Now," Mr. Moss returned to the matter at hand, "get to class on time."

They went off in opposite directions, but Charles stopped and turned around as he remembered. "Mr. Moss!" he cried out. "My first cross-country meet is this Friday."

"I'll be there," Mr. Moss assured the boy.

The first day of a new school year was probably one of the easiest, well, at least for the teachers. The kids were normally more subdued, most likely still feeling shocked that their summer vacation was over. Brendan's first day this year was almost a replay of preceding years. He introduced himself to the new students, went through the names on the class roster, made seating charts, and told the same opening day jokes.

His philosophy was that learning should be an enjoyable experience for his students. School was supposed to be fun! But too many young people came to him with a perverted sense of fun. He knew that he would soon be dealing with students who would be disrupting the lecture and attacking their peers and teachers.

When the day was through, Brendan Moss sat alone in his room and let his mind wander to a familiar place: the past. *Teaching wasn't always this way.*

He had been thirty years old that August. At the time, the last thing he had wanted to do with his life was be a math teacher. He had only majored in math because he was good at it. Back in high school he had had a math teacher named Louis Piccolo who had inspired him to do well. It was Mr. Piccolo who had encouraged Brendan to major in mathematics at St. Francis College in Pennsylvania.

Following his college graduation in 1974 with a Bachelor of Arts in mathematics, twenty-three year old Brendan Moss had left St. Francis with a conviction: He did not want to be a school teacher! He was going to be an author, sell lots of books, and never lay eyes on an equation again.

Six-and-a-half years later, he was delivering pizza and saving his tips so that he could afford a summer house at the Jersey Shore, when his mother told him about a job opening at South Hunterdon High School in Lambertville, New Jersey.

"Just go for the interview," she begged her oldest son.

"I'll go," Brendan promised, "but I don't want to be a teacher."

As he sat waiting for his interview, Brendan hoped that whoever saw him would swiftly recognize that Brendan was not seriously interested in the position and let him go back to his dream of writing all summer at the beach.

"The principal will see you now," the school secretary informed him.

Well, here goes.

When Brendan entered the room, the principal was on the phone and had his back turned.

"Okay," said an oddly familiar voice, "I'll get back to you later."

The principal at South Hunterdon High School whirled around in his chair to face the latest applicant for the open math position.

Brendan's jaw dropped. It was Mr. Piccolo.

"Brendan Moss!" Lou Piccolo quickly recognized his former protégé. "It's so good to see you."

Brendan's first thought scared himself to death. *I'm going to get this job!* And he did.

Thus began the teaching career of Brendan Moss. Once in the classroom, Brendan discovered that he liked to teach math, enjoyed spending his days with teenagers, and especially liked the idea of being paid during July and August, while he was on vacation! *What's not to like?*

Unfortunately, the position at South Hunterdon proved to be temporary. There was a budget-driven reduction in force, and since Brendan was the new kid on the block, he was the first to go.

Since he learned that he actually enjoyed teaching, he went back to college in the fall to obtain a second certification in English. He figured that a double certification would make him a more valuable commodity to the next school district that hired him.

So Brendan enrolled at Brookdale Community College in Lincroft, New Jersey, to begin studying English. His studies ended, however, by the end of October. A high school in Warren, New Jersey called Watchung Hills had obtained his name and number, and the principal called to offer him a position. "You came highly recommended by Louis Piccolo, the principal from Lambertville. Our need here is desperate. A math teacher has suddenly resigned. Can you start tomorrow?"

Could he start tomorrow? You bet I will!

Picking up instruction in the middle of the semester wasn't easy, but he was a math teacher, and he loved it.

One day he was called to the principal's office.

"You're doing a good job," Mr. Roger Huppert complimented. "I was wondering though, if you would like to help out with the girls' basketball program. We have Ms. Harrison as the varsity coach, but we need someone to handle the junior varsity team. Would you be willing to do that for us?"

Like he had a choice! When you're young, new to the district and untenured, you do just about anything you're asked. He had lost one position already, and he was not about to jeopardize another.

"I'd love to."

"I expected that you would," Mr. Huppert responded with a knowing smile. "I told Ms. Harrison that you would come down to her room at the end of the day. Her room number is 235."

Brendan did not have to be told Emily Harrison's room number. He knew exactly who she was and where she taught. He later wondered, *did he accept the offer to coach the girls' JV basketball team to secure his job, or was there more to it?*

At his very first faculty meeting Brendan had watched as a very lovely blond woman had strolled into the library and had sat down with a group of English teachers.

Emily Harrison.

Now a week later, he was walking towards room 235 to meet her. The door was ajar, and Brendan found the attractive Emily Harrison sitting at her desk busy with paperwork. She dropped her pen to the desk as soon as she saw him enter.

"Hi," she opened.

"Hi. I'm here to be your assistant coach," Brendan answered.

Emily patted the chair next to her desk, "Let's talk."

The opening practice wasn't until four-thirty, so they had plenty of time to chat. They joked about their collective inexperience. Emily was only twenty-three and yet deemed ready to coach at the varsity level, and Brendan, although thirty-one, also did not have any coaching experience.

"We should make quite a team," Emily laughed.

When they were done discussing the x's and o's of basketball, their conversation grew more personal.

"So why did you wait so long to start teaching?"

"I don't know," Brendan replied. "I guess I just wasn't sure what I wanted to do with my life. I like to write novels, so I wanted to be a writer for a time. None of them have been published, but it's something I like to do."

"What do you write about?"

"I consider myself kind of a spiritual philosopher," he answered.

"What do you mean by that?"

"I like to write about life, and God, and how crazy this world we live in can be. My stories border a bit on fantasy, but my philosophy of life is based on reality. Well," he grimaced self-consciously, "at least they're base upon reality as I see it."

She smiled back, and Brendan cleared his throat, breaking the sudden silence, "Listen, I just got hit with this coaching assignment today. I need to go home and get some gym stuff."

"Okay," Emily agreed with a trace of embarrassment, "Go ahead. I'll see you at four-thirty."

Brendan nodded and left.

Was that sweat in the palms of his hands? His mind had whirled with thoughts of this incredible turn of events. He had been unemployed, and now he was teaching high school math, coaching basketball, and dare he say, on the precipice of a romantic relationship?

While Brendan Moss sat at his desk reminiscing about the day he first met his beloved Emily, an important impromptu meeting was taking place in the Riverton Superintendent's office. All the key players were present. Bailey Thompson, Tyler Haden, and the rest of the districts' principals sat around a long oval table. Dan Ross, president of the RTA was also present.

The majority of the meeting centered on the budget, future financial situations, personnel, and the state-mandated APPRs. The discussion of the teacher evaluations was the reason why Dan Ross was invited. Ross listened intently, but offered very little feedback. As far as he was concerned, he was there solely to gather information.

Finally, as the short meeting drew to a close, Bailey Thompson asked a question that raised a few eyebrows. "So who," he directed to Mr. Ross, "has the most longevity within the Riverton district?"

"Brendan Moss," he answered immediately.

Thompson perused the papers in front of him. He paused after turning many pages. His right index finger pointed half-way down one of the pages. "Moss makes nearly seventy-five thousand a year."

They all knew what that meant.

Chapter 3

The first week of basketball practice had been more fun than he had imagined. He had found that he liked the players and enjoyed running the drills, and he had sensed that he had a strong nucleus of hard working girls on the team. It had been an exhilarating experience, and nothing had excited him more than being there with Emily Harrison.

They practiced from 4:30 to 6:30, Monday through Friday, and at nine in the morning on Saturday. Both the varsity and junior varsity girls practiced together. Brendan stepped aside as Emily, the varsity head coach, started each day with ball-control drills, followed by shooting competitions and the application of defensive strategies. Truth was, he knew a little bit more about basketball than the rookie coach, but he kept his tongue tied and his mouth shut, assisting wherever he could.

At the end of the first week, after Saturday's practice, he found himself standing alone in the gymnasium with the very beautiful Emily Harrison.

"Did you play in high school?" she asked him.

Brendan shook his head.

"Not for long," he confessed. "I was too short, too passive, and a poor shooter. Even though I was cut from the team," he felt the need to add, "I never stopped playing or trying to make myself better. I love the game, and after high school I got pretty good. I still play today."

"Do you?"

Brendan had immediately noticed a gleam in her eye. He had watched as Emily walked over to the ball cage, unlocked it, took out a ball, and held it up with one hand pointing towards the basket. "Let's see how good you are," she had challenged seductively.

"Alright," he had accepted the challenge, "but I hope it doesn't ruin our relationship."

Emily had liked his choice of words.

They had a relationship.

By the time the middle of September came around, all hell had broken loose at Riverton Middle School. Kids chronically failed to complete homework, students frequently pushed one another into lockers between classes, and teachers were itching to write up several disciplinary reports. Three teachers in the middle school had already been told to 'f-off', and each verbally offensive child had been given a warning. *Yes, only a warning!* Administration in Riverton was keeping true to their word. The number of detentions was noticeably down. A concerted effort to have the dangerous school label removed was underway. The only problem was, the school was still dangerous!

During the second week of the first semester, three boys had been caught with marijuana in their book bags. All three had been suspended for five days. The police were never notified.

Two seventh graders had made violent threats to their teachers. One had told his history teacher that he was going to shoot her in the head. The other, following a verbal reprimand for throwing chalk at other kids, had screamed that he hated the middle school and was going to blow it up. Both boys had received warnings. *Warnings!*

Brendan could only imagine the interventions in the office.

"Boys," they had probably been told in a stern tone, "you really shouldn't say things like that out loud. Murder is bad and blowing up the school is wrong. Please keep your thoughts to yourself from now on."

Well, maybe he was exaggerating just a bit, but it sometimes felt like the Riverton kids had license to do or say whatever they wanted, only to be warned not to do it again. Is that discipline?

Although he often became frustrated, he had to admit that the vast majority of his students were good kids. Oh, there were always widespread homework issues, but by and large, his students paid attention and were respectful, and even though they tended to be a bit chatty, they were also quick to quiet down when asked. Through the years, his students had generally fared well on the state exam, because most had cared about their lives and had hoped to enjoy a bright future.

It was always the few that caused the problems. Each class he taught contained one or two kids who made teaching hard for him and who made learning more difficult for the other kids. The many conscientious students may have been there to learn, but the few apathetic class members habitually disrupted the learning process. It wasn't right, and dealing with disruptions during the lessons demanded time that teachers didn't often have to give.

"Now what you do to one side of the equation, you must do to the other side." Brendan was teaching the kids how to solve two-step equations. It was a good class. The kids were paying attention, following his explanation, and giving every indication that passing eighth grade mattered to them.

He continued, "First I want you to…"

"Ouch!" a child in the front row cried out.

Mr. Moss stopped.

"What happened, Claire?"

"Zach hit me with a penny," she squealed, rubbing the side of her face. "He's been throwing them at me all period."

Brendan peered sternly at the troublemaker, Zach Gilchrist, and ordered, "Get out!"

Zach didn't even voice a complaint or appeal his innocence. He simply got up, smiled at the rest of the class, and left the room. He was used to it. Mr. Moss threw him out of the room nearly every day.

About three weeks into September, Brendan was called into the office to be reprimanded for an infraction of the disciplinary procedure policy.

"You're in trouble," Tyler Haden, pronounced with a wry smile. "For the last five days you have made Zach Gilchrist stand in the hallway."

"He disrupts instruction daily."

"I understand, but even Zach Gilchrist has a right to an education, and if he's made to stand in the hallway, well then; that right is being denied."

"He disrupts instruction daily!" Brendan repeated.

Haden took a deep breath. "This is something you are going to have to handle, Brendan. You cannot continue to throw some kid out of class every day because he can be a little difficult."

"What about the kids who want to learn?" Brendan tossed back at Haden. "What happens to their right to an education, if I have to spend all my time disciplining Zach Gilchrist?"

Tyler didn't have an answer, so he decided to slightly change the subject. "His mother would like a meeting with you. She will be in today after lunch."

"I'll be there," hurled Brendan.

After lunch Mr. Moss returned to Tyler Haden's office. Across from him sat a very angry young woman. She didn't even look old enough to be the mother of a teenager. Brendan guessed that she was in her late twenties.

The principal sat down beside them. "I've asked you two to be here," Haden summarized, "because we have an apparent personality conflict between your son," he nodded towards the mother, "and Mr. Moss."

A personality conflict? The classification made Brendan a little angry. *When a young man is disrespectful, disruptive, and rude through an entire lesson, it is not because the student and teacher have a personality conflict!* Brendan came to a different conclusion when dealing with kids like Zach Gilchrist. *They weren't brought up right!*

"My son says that you bully him, Mr. Moss," started Ms. Gilchrist, "He says other kids in the class are fooling around too, but you always single out Zach. I know my son is no angel, but that doesn't mean that you have the right to treat him the way you do. He deserves an education. If you keep throwing him out of the room, how is he supposed to get one?"

Brendan had heard it all before. A distraught parent comes in to complain about how their child is being treated unfairly. They come in without facts and without a clue as to just how their darling child behaves. They do not care to hear what their child had done. No, all they want to believe is one thing. It's the teacher's fault! Well, Brendan had listened to enough of this nonsense over the years, and this time he decided, he would respond with the battle cry of his father still ringing in his ears: 'Enough is enough'!

"Zach is not here to learn," Brendan answered. "In fact, he's made every effort to prevent other children from learning too. My job is to share information about math. These eighth graders will be taking an important state exam this spring, and it's my responsibility to get them ready for it. Zach is trying to stop me. Your son's behavior has had a negative influence on the other students in my classroom. I agree that he has a right to an education, but when he abuses that right, I have other students to consider. Many of the other students want to learn. They care about their lives. Zach is selfish. All he seems to care about is Zach. What truly amazes me," Brendan was growing a little more agitated, "is that you, his mother, instead of dealing with his behavioral issues at home, have the nerve to come in here and complain about me. Give me a break!"

"Okay, that's enough," Principal Haden interrupted.

Haden dreaded all confrontations between a parent and one of his teachers, and in this case, he was especially uncomfortable. Brendan Moss was not complying with an unspoken standard for parent-teacher conferences. The parent had permission to vent, insult, accuse, and verbally assault members of the staff. The teacher's job was to sit there and take it.

"Mr. Moss, I would like for Zach Gilchrist to remain in class so that he has the opportunity to learn. If there are any difficulties, then I ask that I be summoned to deal with the situation. That way, I can take Zach to the office to calm him down and then return him to class when the problem has been resolved." He turned to the boy's mother. "Is that all right with you?"

"Well," she sighed indignantly, "I don't see where that's going to change anything."

Neither did Brendan.

"This man," she pointed at Mr. Moss, "does not like my son and probably never will. Did you hear the way he spoke to me? I think he's the one who should be punished! I don't trust him. Isn't he too old to still be teaching? How can these kids relate to a man his age? I know my Zach can be difficult, but this Mr. Moss seems so set in his ways that any hope of change on his part is impossible!"

Once again, Tyler Haden jumped in to calm the rising storm. Ever the politician, the principal sensed that this discussion was only heading for trouble. There was one thing that Haden knew for sure. If he didn't put an end to this tirade right now, his eighth grade math teacher was really going to let this mother have it!

A day after the meeting in Mr. Haden's office, the superintendent was visited by the angry mother.

"Something needs to be done!" She complained. "My son is being deprived of his education by that man. He's a dictator! I believe that man should be punished."

"Why did you come to me?" Mr. Thompson wondered.

"I don't believe that Mr. Haden is going to do anything about this. Mr. Moss yelled at me and treated me like he does his students. I don't deserve that."

"I'm not signing this." Brendan automatically protested when the written reprimand was slid across the desk towards him.

"You have to sign it," Haden admonished. "I was ordered by the superintendent to write up a full reprimand for your personal file. Listen Brendan, you cannot talk to a parent like that. It was unprofessional and unacceptable."

The principal once again slid the sheet towards Mr. Moss.

Brendan stared at it. He could simply sign the piece of paper and be done with it. The problem was that this mess was all political. He was innocent. A parent comes in, is told the truth about their child, but stalks out because the truth hurts.

By signing his name to the document, he was basically confessing his fault and acknowledging blame. The signed report would go into his file where it could be used against him at any time. If he were to choose not to sign, it could read as insubordination, which could lead to a suspension or dismissal. Brendan was not in a position to let that happen. Jonathan, his youngest son, would still need to have money for four years of college. There was no way he could afford to lose his job.

Brendan looked up at Tyler Haden, reached for the pen, and signed his name at the bottom of the sheet. A feeling of self-loathing overcame him, as he pushed the sheet back to the principal. It was wrong. He was not guilty of anything.

Brendan had always considered himself a competitor. In sports he fought to the finish. He tried to stand up for what was right. He was disgusted by this feeling that he had somehow failed to compete. He surrendered, because he had to. He signed for his kids. They needed a father who had a job.

What would Emily have thought?

"That's 10-8!" Brendan had boasted.

"It's not over yet," Emily had breathed heavily, winded by the one-on-one contest. "Loser buys lunch."

Brendan liked challenges, and he especially enjoyed being challenged athletically. But when it came to dating, Brendan Moss was the man, and he was going to pay!

For the next five minutes, Brendan did his best to look like he was playing hard and trying to win, but he took careful effort to purposely miss his shots. He still made Emily Harrison work for her points, but when the game ended, Emily was on top, 12-10.

After they had unlaced their sneakers, Emily had gathered her things and headed towards the girls' locker room. About to enter, she had looked back at Brendan and smiled.

"I knew that would work."

With his sixth period class busy on the room assignment, Brendan went about assisting those in need of extra help and checking the papers of those who claimed to be finished. One girl in the back of the room had not even lifted her pencil.

"Cali?" Mr. Moss addressed her firmly. "Why isn't any of this work done?"

No response.

Every other student in the class was working on the problem on the board. It always made Brendan wonder, *how can a teenager think that it's okay to just sit there and do nothing, while all the other kids work? Who did they think they were?*

"If you do not want to work in class, then you will not be enjoying your lunch period with your friends today. Do you understand?"

It was almost noon, and sixty year old Brendan Moss was assigned to yet another lunch duty.

"Shouldn't I be exempt from lunch duty because of my age?" he would often joke with a colleague.

The response was always the same. "You're good at this duty. The kids are afraid of you!"

If a student felt like misbehaving, he would force the offender to stand against the wall outside of the cafeteria and wait until they were the last in line to eat. On occasion, if the actions of the child were particularly offensive, he made him or her eat his or her lunch on the wall as well. Brendan was always careful to make sure that all the kids got to eat. Preventing a kid from eating lunch would mean big trouble. Making them wait a while was still legal. The kids hated this particular form of discipline. It meant that they could not sit and talk to their friends. It was an effective punishment. Usually, an offender instantly improved his or her behavior, because he or she didn't want to stand out in the hall for two days in a row.

"Cali!" Mr. Moss cried out once he spotted the girl. "Come over here," he motioned with his hand.

Cali Evans did not move.

"Here!" Mr. Moss indicated more sternly.

Cali Evans continued to ignore him.

Brendan moved towards her. He knew that she had heard him and that she knew exactly what he wanted.

"I'm not standing on the wall," Cali defied.

"Well," Mr. Moss fired, "then I guess you're going to lunch detention."

The young spitfire whirled on her heels and began to walk away.

Mr. Moss followed.

"Where do you think you're going?" he called.

"I'm going to the office," Cali shot back.

This was not the first time Brendan had heard that pout. He always found it so interesting. When he was a kid, going to the office was a big uh-oh. It was like going to prison. The principal was the last person any kid wanted to see, and even worse than facing the principal was the realization that any information relayed home meant even bigger trouble.

Nowadays, they went to the office to tell on the teacher! *My, how things have changed!*

At Riverton Middle School, the office was not a place a kid feared. It was a haven, a place where counselors and social workers alike were there to wrap their arms around any misbehaving child and rescue them from the big, bad teachers. Brendan could not even begin to count how many times a defiant child had refused to accept his or her just punishment and cried out, "I'm going to the office".

So as Cali Evans stomped away, Brendan informed the other lunch monitor that he was going to follow. By the time Cali Evans reached the office her reddened face was flushed with tears. She went right up to one of the secretaries and cried out dramatically, "I need to see Mr. Haden."

After years of dealing with disrespectful and disobedient students, Mr. Moss was acutely familiar with all the acts of righteous indignation, yet it never ceased to amaze him how the office staff always appeared aghast when a raging student stomped through the door. He imagined they were thinking, "How could anyone treat a poor child this way?" He would watch the fake tears fall and each time wonder, *how do they make themselves cry like that?*

What Moss did know was this. When all the dust cleared after Cali's dramatic performance, she would receive a pardon and only one person would be left to reprimand: him!

After a couple of minutes Missy Franklin, head of the middle school guidance department, emerged from down the office hallway with Cali Evans at her side.

"I'm going to let Cali go down and get her lunch," Missy Franklin insisted. "Then she can come back and have lunch with me."

"Okay," Brendan retaliated, "but the punishment still stands. Tomorrow she eats out in the hallway of the cafeteria."

Later that same afternoon, Brendan stood outside in the hall between classes. Just as the next period was about to begin, Tyler Haden came walking towards him. Brendan was joking around with a student, when the principal stopped in front of him. As he waved the kid into the room, Brendan could only wonder: *What now?*

Haden got right to the point. "I don't want students standing in the hallway during lunch. I realize it's been an effective form of punishment, but you're going to need to come up with something else."

Brendan didn't move.

"I think it looks bad for the high school students passing by to see our kids singled out for poor behavior."

Uh, the same high school kids who used to be put on the wall in the past?

"I don't like the whole public display of it. So," Haden continued, "if you need to punish during cafeteria time, I would appreciate it if you would write them up, and we will put them in lunch detention."

"Lunch detention with Missy Franklin, while they watch TV?" Brendan could not resist the dig.

Haden ignored the sarcasm. "Yesterday," he resumed as if he hadn't heard his eighth grade math teacher, "you put Donald Allison on the wall, and you later wrote him up, claiming that he annoys you. That's what you wrote, Brendan. There is nothing specific in the report detailing what the kid did or said; only that he annoys you."

"A potential food fight was about to start at another table." Brendan swiftly defended. "I was in a bit of a hurry, so I quickly generalized the situation with Donald Allison so the office staff would have an idea as to why he was there. I agree I should have explained his behavior more accurately. I'm sorry."

"Anyway," Haden re-seized control of their discussion, "his father was upset over the vagueness of the report and wants to know what his son did to deserve a punishment. He also," the principal held up his hand to prevent Mr. Moss from interrupting, "e-mailed the superintendent, complaining about what you did."

Now it made sense! Eliminating the-against-the wall during lunch punishment was not really about putting misbehaving students on public display. It was because a parent complained!

Riverton was an interesting school district. All rules and behavioral guidelines were subject to change. If a parent complained! For reasons Brendan Moss would probably never understand, the administration was afraid of the parents. When a mother felt like her misbehaving child was punished too harshly, the teachers were usually told to handle the situation differently. *Is your child not receiving enough playing time in their sport? Complain! He or she may just be in the starting lineup next game. It didn't make any sense.*

Brendan's three children had attended the public school in Ashton, about fifteen miles from Riverton. He had requested a meeting once because his son, Matthew, was having some issues with the basketball coach. The principal, coach, and athletic director were polite and respectful, and they had patiently listened to Brendan's opinions, but after the meeting ended, the only thing that had changed was Brendan's realization that it was Matthew's responsibility to change his attitude if he wanted more playing time.

Imagine that. Ashton School District was going to make their students accountable. It can be done! Why wouldn't Riverton do the same?

Before he left school, Brendan went to the middle school office to check his mail. There was only a sticky note left in his box. It read: "Please call the superintendent's office".

"Mr. Thompson's office," a pleasant voice answered Brendan's call.

"Hi, Joyce," Brendan greeted the long-time secretary. "It's Brendan Moss. What's up?"

"Hi, Mr. Moss," Joyce DeHaven answered in her usual friendly tone. "Mr. Thompson would like to meet with you tomorrow at nine."

"Do you know what it's about?"

"I don't."

Silence.

"Alright," Brendan finally responded, "I'll be there at nine."

He hung up and returned to his room. His instincts were on overdrive. This was not good.

Once a month the math department at Riverton held a meeting over in the high school. Due to recent budget cuts and the financial decision not to replace retired teachers, there were only four math teachers remaining in the district. The head of the math department, Rachel Weiss, was already venting by the time Brendan Moss entered the room.

"Testing, testing, and more testing!" She was saying to Barbara Gagne who taught ninth graders. "Now we have to create eight week pre-tests to prepare for a state exam which no one has seen."

"It's crazy." Gagne agreed.

"Administration doesn't know what's going to be on the tests, and apparently even the state doesn't know." Rachel Weiss complained. "Shame on the state leadership in New York! There are no clear expectations, no sample exams to guide teaching, and the standards are so vague. Here Barbara," she slid a packet towards Gagne, "read this standard."

Standards are simply the topics which a teacher is responsible for presenting to their students. It was a list containing all the different things to be taught during the school year leading up to the exam. The problem wasn't the amount of material to be instructed. The problem was the wording of the standards themselves.

Barbara Gagne read the particular standard Rachel Weiss pointed out.

'Informally assess the degree of visual overlap of two numerical distributions with similar variables, measuring the difference between the centers by expressing it as a multiple of a measure of variability."

Gagne had to smile.

"What is it saying?"

Rachel shrugged. "Look at how difficult the wording is. I don't even know what it means and I'm the teacher!" She laughed. "So how am I to figure out instruction? 'Visual overlap of two numerical data distribution'? What egghead in Albany wrote that? It would be great if the state would just tell us what to teach. I wish they would give us clear guidelines. I'd be happy to teach if I knew what it was they wanted. What's with all the espionage and secrecy? I don't get it."

Moss quietly sat down and listened. He too sympathized with the ladies' frustration. He was frustrated by the absence of clear expectations also.

"Here's the problem." Mrs. June LaCroix, who taught the upper level math classes pined. "Many of our children in Riverton have difficulty reading. We're not like other districts in the area. We have students whose parents are in jail, or alcoholics, and so many parents today don't even read to their kids anymore. Our unemployment is over 70%."

"There's going to be so much more reading to do on the exam." Rachel Weiss concurred. "Our students have to be able to read the problem before they can even begin to do the math. And not only can't a portion of our kids read, but so many don't even want to learn."

"Tell me about it." Brendan chimed in. "I've got this kid named Zach Gilchrist who disrupts instruction daily."

"I've got his older brother." Rachel Wilson frowned. " I heard from their school social worker that there is absolutely no supervision at home. So how are we expected to deal with them? You can't touch them and administration gets upset if you scold them. Our hands are tied."

"Yet," Brendan added, "these are the same parents who come in and complain. They don't attend parent-teacher conferences, and never respond when you leave a message concerning their child's behavior. But boy," he laughed, "try handing out discipline to their kids and they stomp in here ready to fight! And the worst part is the way Riverton's administration coddles to these parents. Usually I get in more trouble than the kid because my scolding may have hurt their feelings."

"We don't hurt their feelings." Barbara Gagne ventured her opinion. "These kids are sly. They know how to push a teacher's buttons and get us to say the wrong thing. What some of these kids do is plain evil."

"It's just Riverton."

Moss and the other women turned to look at June LaCroix.

"Do you think Ashton would be afraid of these parents? You know what I'm talking about, Brendan; your kids go there."

Brendan nodded.

"When kids from other districts are asked to leave because of their behavior, we're the only school in the area who welcomes these rabble-rousers with open arms. And then these same children can't pass a state exam and we get blamed. We have lots of kids who like and want to learn but the 'Zachs' of the world make it difficult for everybody."

For a long moment no one spoke. It wasn't until Rachel Weiss, the department head, cleared her throat and introduced the main topic for this month's meeting that anyone said or added anything.

"Well," she sighed, "here's the next piece of bad news, guys. Albany has added a new dimension to our personal teacher evaluation. Not only do we have to create tests which mirror an exam we're not allowed to see, but now the kids are going to take a computerized test in the seventh and eighth grade.

"Arrangements will be made for these students to use the computers in the library to take this test. Then later in the year, the kids will take the test again to show some level of improvement. And as always, it is not the child who is being mathematically evaluated, but rather the teacher who either achieved or failed to deliver the instruction."

"What's the test for?" Moss asked.

"No one knows."

"I think they're out to get us." Brendan couldn't resist making his opinion known.

Rachel Weiss pursed her lips.

"You're probably right."

Chapter 4

He had felt confident. He had expected Emily Harrison to say yes. He was also nervous, jittery even. What if she said no? She would say yes. Wouldn't she?

They'd already had one lunch together, the day they had played one-on-one. That was awesome, but since then, outside of a few bus rides and sitting together on the bench, well, it wasn't like they were dating.

The evening's game had been canceled due to the weather, and there was only one thing Brendan wished to do with his free night. Emily Harrison was still in her room preparing for next week's classes when he walked in. He had begun making a habit of entering unannounced. It seemed like she liked that. Somehow that meant something.

"It's too bad about the game tonight," Brendan stammered nervously. "I really wanted to play those guys."

"I know," Emily returned. "I really wanted to play tonight too."

"Listen," Brendan tried to maintain his composure, "I was thinking. Since there's no game tonight and the roads are recently cleared, what do you think about coming to the Sabres game with me? I've got two tickets and..."

"I'd love to go!"

Wow! She said yes!

"I thought maybe," he was still a bit apprehensive about asking for more, "We could leave around four, and maybe get some dinner before the game."

"I'd love to."

Well, I guess that was that!

"I don't know where you live," Brendan said, although it was a white lie. He knew exactly where her apartment was and had driven by it numerous times, hoping seeing her there.

Emily had given him her address.

"See you at four?"

"Okay," she smiled. "See you at four."

"Dad! Dad!"

Jonathan Moss had no idea where his father's mind was at the moment, but the Ashton High senior knew one thing for sure. His Dad was in a dream world.

"Huh?" Brendan finally acknowledged his son.

"See you at four?"

"Yeah. Yeah. I'll be there."

Jonathan played sweeper on the boys' varsity soccer team, and his game today was at four. The senior-laden team held high expectations for the season and were already six and zero. Brendan rarely missed any game that any of his three children were involved in.

"What am I going to do with my life when there are no more games to watch?"

"You'll have grandchildren," a friend once suggested in reply.

Grandchildren! Emily would have loved grandchildren.

"Northwestern beat you guys last time," Brendan reminded his son.

"That was last year."

Brendan had taken the day off from school today. He wasn't ill, but he was starting to feel stressed by the situation in Riverton, and he decided that it would be best if he took some time away. A day would do. After thirty years on the job, Brendan had accumulated hundreds of sick days.

Many years he had perfect attendance, and most years he missed less than a day or two.

Brendan chose this specific day as a sick day, because the drive to Jonathan's away game at Northwestern High School was over an hour long. A few years back, when Amanda and Matthew had played high school sports, the games were much closer. During the past couple of years however, many of the leagues had disbanded due to the multiple mergers of districts. These mergers always meant that many teachers would be losing their jobs, especially those young, energetic ones, and finding other positions wasn't easy in the current market.

Ashton High School decided not merge with other towns, and enrollment did not change. Since they were a small school, they would continue to compete against other small schools. This occasionally resulted in an increase in distance between competing schools, but Brendan really didn't care. A game was a game as far as he was concerned. His son was playing, and he would be there watching. The length of the drive didn't matter.

As was his usual habit, he stood against the fence down by the goal where his boy would be playing defense. Although he stood by himself, Brendan half-pretended that his Emily stood beside him, so that together they could cheer on their youngest child while he played ball. At times, he would even imagine that he was discussing the nuances of the game with her. He would tell her all about the children and how they were doing.

"He's a terrific kid, sweetheart. He's still quiet and shy like you remember, and he has a wonderful circle of friends. They're over at the house all the time. There are five of them. They play ball and video games, and they practically eat us out of house and home. You want to know the truth, sweetheart?" A tiny tear came to his eye as he paused in his pretend conversation. "You did such a good job with all three of them. My God, you should have seen Amanda at the wedding! While Brian's father was performing the service, I thought she was going to leap into the groom's arms right then and there. I never saw her so excited. Later I watched them at the reception together. Amanda and Brian are so in love, so happy, so meant to be together, and so like us! Matthew is struggling a little bit with what he wants to do with his life. He was so close to you. I think it hit him the hardest, but he's a great kid and I certainly am not worried about him, but boy, all four of us could sure use your positive spirit, sound judgment, and loving guidance, and I..."

Score!

Brendan's feet actually left the ground as he pumped his right fist into the air. When the Ashton boys scored a goal he was unable to contain his joy. He looked towards his son to watch for his reaction. Jon ran forward and leaped towards his friend, Zach. The two boys bumped their bodies into one another as a form of celebration.

And why not? Good things in life were meant to be celebrated.

Following the game, which Ashton won 2-0, Brendan congratulated his son and tossed him ten dollars for food with the team at McDonald's. He then climbed into his car and drove home alone, again.

He always seemed to be alone these days.

Myles Langston had had enough! As he stared at his locker, tears streaming down his face, the fourteen year old beat his fists in rage. *How dare they question his manhood! If he had a gun with him right now, he would blow the heads off of Buster McHale and all his bullying football pals. Why couldn't they just leave him alone?*

He was only fourteen, but life was all so confusing. He was painfully thin, his face bombarded by acne, and he was probably the most uncoordinated boy in his grade. That didn't mean he was gay!

Yeah, he wasn't completely sure about his sexuality. Girls certainly didn't interest him, and the boys were not an attraction either, at least he didn't think so. All Myles knew was this: He was different. He was the only child of Methodist Pastor, Ronald Langston, and his wife Rae, and even though he was raised in a Christian home, there was something about the Bible that gnawed at him. It seemed so preferential. It looked to him like the Bible was only for normal people, that God did play favorites and that unfortunately, he was not on the right team.

This morning had started out like any other day at Riverton High. He no longer rode the bus to school, because the fifteen minutes of verbal and physical harassment had become too much to bear. For the past two years, he had not been able to find a seat, because the other kids, boys and girls alike, would either put their feet up on the seat to block Myles or tell him that there was no way he was sitting next to them. The annoyed bus driver had been forced to pull over and order a youngster to lift their feet so "Myles can sit, and we can all finally get to school". At times Myles had wondered just who the bus driver was annoyed with.

Even safely seated, the much bullied Myles Langston had been forced to endure further humiliation and teasing as the bus ride resumed. Kids would poke at him, some with a great deal of force; while others had taunted him with rude gestures and slurs. "Gay", "faggot", and "homo", were spit into his ears, and the day usually wouldn't get much better once the bus arrived at school.

Since the beginning of the school year, Myles' mother escorted her son to and from school each day. It was the best and most loving thing she could think to do. It was also the most painful.

Rae Langston would stop the car near the front sidewalk, and wish her child a good day. Then she would sit and watch to see if anything would happen. One morning, she watched as a bigger boy wearing a Riverton football jersey pushed Myles, almost causing her son to lose his balance. On another afternoon, as she waited to pick her child up, she saw Myles sprinting towards her while three larger girls stood at the main entrance laughing and pointing. Her son got into the car red-faced, and as Rae watched her sons eyes fill with tears, she herself needed to fight back her own tears. The bullying didn't take place all that often, but it occurred enough to break her heart.

Why? Myles was such a nice boy. He wouldn't hurt a fly. Why did the other children have to be so mean? Why do they treat him that way? Why do Ronald and I keep taking him back here to be tormented, ridiculed, and abused?

"He needs to learn how to defend himself," Ronald had repeated. "Myles needs to stand up for himself, and draw a line in the sand."

At eighty-five pounds? How, my dear husband, how?

The pitiful scenes repeated often enough. *What were her options? Should she jump out of her car and chastise the hooligans? Oh my God, Myles would be so embarrassed if she ever did that. No, her position was already determined. She would have to sit there, say nothing, do nothing, and do her best to settle herself as her sobs overcame her.*

Rae and her husband had made an appointment last year with the middle school principal, Tyler Haden. The meeting had gone well. Mr. Haden had listened, cared, sympathized, and promised to look into the situation, but the bullying had never stopped.

After Myles had moved to the high school, the Langston family had hoped that there would be an improvement in supervision. There hadn't been. The Riverton High School was not a safe haven for the outcasts either. In fact, things appeared to be getting worse.

"Hey faggot. Are you crying again? Look gay-boy, I need money for lunch. Give me what you've got."

"You are such a loser!"

Buster McHale quickly spun around to see where the voice came from. Myles managed a small smile, as his only friend Charles Hayes stood in the center of the hallway near Myles locker.

"You know what?" Buster shouted, "I'm going to kick your ass right after school today."

"Is that right?" inquired a different voice.

Mr. Moss!

"I'm really getting sick of you too!" McHale spewed. "Why don't you just go back to the middle school where you belong? You're not wanted over here."

Brendan Moss smiled. Only it was not a smile of joy. Moss turned to look at Myles and Charles. "Go to class boys. I will deal with Mr. McHale."

He turned back to face Riverton's biggest bully, "Come with me."

Brendan was only over in the high school because he was on his way to his meeting with the superintendent, Bailey Thompson, and he was not happy about having to intercept Buster McHale along the way. McHale was a junior this year. He was a star athlete in football, basketball, and baseball, and maybe for that very reason, considered an untouchable by the administration. Brendan doubted that the boy would be reprimanded, but part of his job was to protect the kids. This included protecting them from bullies like McHale, and whether the bully got punished or not was completely out of his hands. Administrative inconsistency was not his problem. He would fulfill his responsibility and report the incident.

The Riverton High School offices had been recently reconstructed. New rooms, two refurbished gymnasiums, and a handful of other reconstructing projects were still underway. Riverton offered every child everything he or she could ever hope for in an educational setting, and it was rarely appreciated by the children the school was built for.

"I'd like to see Mr. Dowling," Brendan informed the office secretary. He motioned to Buster McHale, "Have a seat on the bench."

McHale ignored the request.

"Have a seat!" Mr. Moss repeated quite loudly. There was still no response from the boy.

The assistant principal poked his head out of the door, "Come in, Mr. Moss." He motioned to Buster McHale. "You too."

Jeff Dowling, the assistant principal at Riverton High, was still a relatively young man. Dowling was in his early forties, sprouted a short beard, and had a kind face. He was used to commotion outside his office door. With the door partially open, he had easily overheard Mr. Moss' loud command to Buster McHale.

"Have a seat, gentlemen."

Brendan sat down. McHale did not.

"So what seems to be the trouble?"

"As I was walking past a couple of students, I overheard Buster telling Charles Hayes that he was going to kick his ass after school today."

Jeff Dowling leaned back in his chair.

"Is that true, Buster?"

"He called me a loser!" McHale said in his best pout. "It hurt my feelings."

"All right," Dowling sighed, "I get the picture. You are twice the size of Charles. Leave the kid alone." The assistant principal paused. "We will not tolerate bullying here at Riverton. Go back to class."

And that was that. Well, Mr. Dowling still had something else to add.

"Who do you guys think you'll meet in the sectionals?" Mr. Dowling wanted to talk football.

"We're hoping it's going to be Sommerville," Buster answered amiably, and as he did so he stole a glance at Mr. Moss, as if to say, 'Don't you know who you're dealing with? I'm captain of the football team'.

Buster left the office, whistling a tune as he went. Brendan could only sit and stare at Jeff Dowling as if he were looking at a ghost.

"Is there anything else, Mr. Moss?"

Is there anything else? This big punk taunts the smaller kids daily, physically assaults them when no adults are looking, and all you can come up with is the playoff schedule?

Brendan knew that the best thing to do would be to politely excuse himself and be on his way. That would have been the best thing, the wisest thing, and the most sensible course of action to take, but he was fuming!

"That young hooligan gets away with murder!" he spat at the assistant principal, "But no one seems to care as long as he terrorizes quarterbacks and dunks a basketball. He can do whatever he wants. I'm sick of it! I'm going to make a prediction, Jeff. One of these days someone is going to get hurt, and get hurt badly. I can smell a tragedy on the horizon, and it will be something that didn't need to happen. We could have stopped it, but we chose winning football games instead."

With that, Brendan left the assistant principal's office. He exited so swiftly that Jeff Dowling could not reply.

Brendan next moved down the long hallway to the superintendent's office. He had some suspicions concerning the content of this next meeting. First, he'd had the run-in with Zach Gilchrist's mother, and then there was the cafeteria incident with Cali Evans. *Maybe he had taken things too far, but was administration taking it far enough?*

The superintendent's office was tucked in the back corner of the high school. After making it down the long hallway, Brendan had to turn a corner, and then stroll by another conglomerate of offices. Right beyond the business manager's cubicle was the reception area for the superintendent. Brendan was greeted by Bailey Thompson's personal secretary and told that the superintendent would see him soon.

After about a three minute wait, Mr. Moss entered the most spacious room in the newly-renovated building complex. Bailey Thompson stood from behind his desk and stretched out his hand. The two men had never met, and both hoped to at least make a good first impression. Brendan had only seen Thompson from a distance during the first-day-of-school introduction in the auditorium. The man was a lot shorter than Brendan had initially perceived. The superintendent looked to be in his forties, with brown hair and dark brown eyes. He welcomed Brendan in with a big, friendly smile.

"Mr. Moss!" Thompson cried out, a bit too theatrically. "Please have a seat. I have some things I hoped to discuss with you."

Brendan did as instructed.

"I'm going to get right to the point."

Brendan already surmised that this meeting was not going to go well.

"At Tuesday's Board of Education meeting," Mr. Thompson began to explain, "we discovered that our deficit for the following school year is around two million dollars. That's a lot of money! At the present moment, I am struggling to find a way to cut two million out of the budget. Obviously, our greatest expense is personnel. That's why," Thompson gulped nervously, "I called you in today."

Moss kept silent, but his heart was pounding furiously.

"You have been with the Riverton School District for twenty-seven years now, Mr. Moss. Your tenure here is not the longest of the staff, as I initially thought, but regardless; you are the oldest in age, and for some reason make the most money, in the entire district I might add." Bailey Thompson's own curiosity interrupted his train of thought. "Why is that?"

"I taught high school math in New Jersey for three years before my wife and I relocated here in Western New York," Brendan informed him. "For some reason my starting salary was based on what I was paid in New Jersey. This made me a very well paid first year teacher. I never asked why, so I have no idea what happened. Since then my salary has increased according to contract." Now it was Brendan's turn to be the inquisitor. "Why do you ask?"

Thompson fidgeted in his chair. He didn't like the question.

"You've been here a long time, Mr. Moss. My records show that you will be sixty-one this coming March. This is a tough town to teach in. The kids can be difficult, and like all of us," he grimaced, "you've probably thought about retirement for quite some time now. Am I right?"

Brendan's expression revealed nothing. He decided he was not going to answer that question.

"The deficit puts me in a very tenuous position," Bailey Thompson resumed. "I need to make personnel cuts. If it comes down to it, a sizeable chunk of our staff is going to lose their jobs. We've got a relatively young staff, Brendan." That was the first time he called Mr. Moss by his first name. "They are people with young families, struggling to start a life. I'd hate to see them lose their jobs, especially during this challenging recession. Finding another position in a different school district wouldn't be easy, which brings me to you."

Brendan politely let the man have his say. He already knew where this was heading.

"You're sixty years old. You've had a good career, raised a family, and I suspect that you've put money aside for the future."

"I have a seventeen year old at home," Brendan interrupted.

"Oh, I didn't know that." He didn't. Bailey Thompson knew Brendan Moss' age and knew that the man's wife had died a short time ago. That was the extent of his research. "I have thrown together a couple of retirement packages for you to consider. They are loaded with incentives that just might interest you."

Brendan could barely believe the nerve of the man. This was his life, his career, and he would be the one to decide when he was done with it.

Brendan interpreted the silent period as the sign that it was his turn to speak. "Let me be as respectful as possible. I feel as badly as anyone else for the economic crisis New York State is in. I know that this recession has adversely affected lots of people, and it certainly bothers me that this crisis has trickled down to the public school system. I really am sympathetic, but understand this: I'm not the one responsible for excess spending, or the poor real estate market, or all of the defaulted loans, and since I wasn't the cause of the damage, please don't expect me to be the fall guy. I work hard and I work honestly." Brendan held up his hand, as he detected that the superintendent was going to apologize for insinuating his math teacher's work ethic was not up to par. "And yes, I have made wise use of my finances, while our state government has not, so my future does appear secure. By the way, I also have a family to support. I do have a grown up daughter who is married, but I'm still providing food and shelter for a twenty-one year old who's in college, and a seventeen year old senior in high school. I need to work. My family needs money too. But I don't want you to think that I'm not retiring because I need the money. I'm not retiring, because I don't want to!" Brendan looked right into Thompson's eyes. "I like this job. I still enjoy coming to work every day, and when I'm ready to leave, I'll decide when, I'll decide how, and I'll let you know."

"Let me present it to you in a different light. Your test scores for the past two years have been slightly below the acceptable goals set here at Riverton."

This response piqued Moss' interest.

Thompson continued, "We're already designated as a school in review for our low English scores, and I don't want the same label to burden our math department, simply because the eighth grade teacher cannot raise the test scores."

"Are you blaming me for my students' failures?"

The superintendent was prepared to share his perspective. He leaned forward, as his elbows rested on the desk, "Listen Mr. Moss, no one in Riverton is blaming anyone for our students failure to measure up. I'm not a math teacher, so I don't have helpful hints to share, but I do know this," he paused to stress his point, "other math teachers, from other school districts, are getting the job done." Bailey Thompson stopped again for effect. "You're not!"

Moss couldn't help himself. He rose from his seated position across from the superintendent and roughly pushed his chair behind him. "Let me give you some reality, pal. I teach the Standards as the State of New York outlines them. I implement them into instruction and teach my students everything they are supposed to be tested on. I teach everything well, and the kids learn it, but then when the test comes out, the wording is confusing, questions are deliberately tricky, and in many ways it is their reading ability more than their math skills that is tested. Many of our students already struggle with reading. Our school is being unfairly compared with other districts, where children come from more stable households. By the way," Brendan moved back as he calmed himself, "my failing students have a record of excessive unexcused absences, in- school-suspension, and full suspension. Our school is almost 70% low income and a good portion of our students are on reduced lunch fees. Our kids have parents on drugs, alcoholics, and some have even spent time in jail. And on top of that, some of our students don't live with their parents or live in foster homes. It's not fair to judge teachers in Riverton the way you might evaluate teachers from upscale Williamsville. I will not be held responsible for these kids. Besides, in the last two years the State has taken the liberty of putting in question types that are not even on the standards! If Albany doesn't tell me to teach a particular topic, but then turns around and tests the kids on what I was not told to teach, then how am I to deal with that? Is it my fault, because I can't read minds? It's like the State Education Department is trying to…"

It was like someone suddenly snapped open a window blind. Brendan's mind began racing with impressions, conjectures, and eye-opening clarity. *That was exactly it! Albany wanted the kids to fail! Oh, it wasn't because they were against the children or anything bizarre like that, no; it was the teachers they wished to discredit.* It was now becoming clear to Brendan.

When he had first started in education, individual school districts had held themselves to a high but reasonable level of accountability. Today these self-imposed standards were being enforced by the State of New York. *Why the change?* It was a game of "follow the money".

Why the teachers had become the primary target was still a mystery. Parents certainly blamed us, and Albany seemed to be on a mission to prove that they were justified in doing so. Excessive absences, poor behavior, and lack of effort were dismissed as probable causes of failure. It was the school teacher's fault, and Albany was going to prove it! That way, the security of a teacher's right to tenure could be challenged. Everyone suspected that all along, that was Albany's goal. The State hoped to blame the teachers for failing students and begin the process of removing a teacher's right to lifetime tenure.

"Mr. Moss, regardless of how the State Tests are presented, Riverton is lagging behind many other school districts. You are the eighth grade…"

As soon as the thought hit him, Brendan verbalized his insight.

"The State has the money for schools, doesn't it?"

The look on the superintendent's face was telling.

"They have it, and could give it to us, but they don't wish to ease our financial burden. I'm right, am I not? By withholding the money, they can make things worse for us: fewer teachers, bigger classrooms, and less control. Blame the teacher. They can't fire us so…"

Thompson stood, "You know Mr. Moss. I can make things very difficult for you around here. You may think your tenure protects you, or that some powerful teachers' union is going to stand by your side, but here's what I say; the RTA will not support you. Your local association is only as strong as its weakest link. Oh, you'll still have a position here at Riverton. I can't do anything about that yet, but there will be changes," Thompson paused, "and you may not like them."

Brendan Moss lowered his head in farewell, but he couldn't resist one last jab. "We'll see."

Chapter 5

"Are you ready for this?"

"She's what I live for," Brendan had answered his brother's question firmly. "I'm going to be good at this. There's only one thing I want on the planet earth, and it's Emily." Brendan had smiled at his younger brother. "You just be the best man. I'll handle the husband part."

He had never felt more confident that he was doing the right thing in his entire life. As he and his brother stood together at the front of the church, Brendan's attention remained on the back of the church. Soon, his bride Emily would be standing there, about to be delivered forever to her groom. Brendan had no doubt that he and the future Mrs. Emily Moss would be a forever thing. God made her for him.

There she was! As he stared at her standing beside her father, Brendan remembered the day that they got engaged.

It was just a year ago. By this point, they had been dating a little over two years, and on the day that he had proposed, they were again playing one-on-one basketball. The score was tied at 10-10, and Brendan knew that now was the time.

He cradled the ball in his armpit, let his body relax, and signaled to Emily that he needed a time-out.

"Winner decides where we go for our honeymoon," he declared.

"Are you asking me to marry you?" she asked, shocked.

"You bet I am."

From out of his gym short's pocket, he had removed a small box that he had kept hidden while he played. He had had the box with him for the past week, just in case he felt the time was right, and at this moment he knew it was. He had fallen to his knees, opened the lid of the box, and held the ring out towards her.

"Will you marry me?"

He sat alone on his bed, leafing through the photograph albums. It was an old habit that he couldn't seem to break. Brendan couldn't resist peeking at the album that was the most dear to him. The date July 18th, 1986, was embossed in gold on the cover. He opened to the first picture and let his hand softly trace along her body. There were so many pictures and so many memories. Even now, he felt so grateful for the twenty years that he was married to Emily.

The pain of losing her was lessening. He still hurt, but he could function. Even with his everlasting heartache, Brendan Moss couldn't bring himself to shake his fist at the Lord and cry out in despair, "why me"? No, instead he could only bow his head, and with deep reverence utter the same words in a different tone.

"Why me Lord? How could You be so good to me?"

Myles Langston had suffered through the usual taunting and teasing during gym class. He stood in front of his locker, reapplying his school clothes to his frail little body when he was hit in the back of the neck with a rolled up magazine. The magazine was in the hands of Buster McHale and featured a suggestively posed naked man on the cover.

"Here you go gay-boy," McHale pushed the nude photograph against his face. A handful of McHale's cohorts swarmed around Myles's locker. Two stood to the back, scanning the locker room for coaches. Other kids, nicer boys, quietly took off their gym clothes and put on their normal class wear. One by one, these boys, too scared to interfere with the harassment, left to return to class.

Myles was left alone to fend for himself against his much larger tormentors.

"Are the pictures not good enough?" Buster McHale mocked. "Then maybe this will excite you."

Buster ripped off his t-shirt and gym shorts and pressed himself against Myles.

"Do you like this better?"

His attempt at humor did not have the effect he was hoping for. As he stood totally exposed, his gang of henchmen looked back and forth at one another with a faint expression of horror. This was not something they wanted to see either.

"I'm out of here!" one of the football boys said to the guy beside him. "This is getting too weird."

In seconds, only Myles Langston and Buster McHale remained in the boys' locker room. Myles crumbled to the floor, and with his face held in his hands, sobbed uncontrollably.

"You made a fool out of me!" Buster screamed as he reached down and lifted poor, defenseless Myles Langston to his feet. With an open hand he struck Langston hard across the face. The sound reverberated throughout the locker room, and Myles slumped back to the floor.

"It figures," Buster heard a voice call from behind him. "You hit like a girl."

Charles Hayes had been rummaging frantically through his locker a few minutes before the locker room attack on Myles Langston. He was looking for his social studies report on Ancient Egypt. He had just had it! He had been excused from gym class earlier in the morning due to a cross-country meet after school. So instead of playing touch football with the other boys in his class, he had sat at a table in the gym, re-reading his report. He put it...

Then he remembered. He had gone to talk to Mr. Lyons, the gym teacher, while his classmates were changing. He had probably left the report on a table in the locker room. Uh-oh! If certain people saw it and recognized that it was his, they were apt to do something to it!

"I left my social studies report in the gym locker room," he told Mrs. McKinney, his social studies teacher, as he stood anxiously outside her door. "Can I go get it?"

As soon as he received permission, Charles hustled down the long hallway towards the gym. He feverishly hoped that his paper was where he had left it and that a bully had not destroyed it. As he was about to enter the locker room, four football players came rushing out.

Two things seemed odd about their exit. For one, they appeared nervous or uneasy about something, and they hurried past him without uttering a single taunt or offering the usual shove. Something was up.

Charles discovered very quickly just what that something was, as he stumbled upon a scene that scared him nearly out of his wits. On the floor, huddled up like a freezing homeless man, was his friend Myles Langston, sobbing like a baby. As frightening as it was to see Myles in this condition, it was even more terrifying to see a naked Buster McHale towering over his friend. Charles watched helplessly as the biggest bully at Riverton grabbed Myles by the collar of his shirt and lifted him up. Charles stood as if frozen in ice, as Buster raised his right hand and slapped Myles across the face. Myles had fallen back to the ground, where he once again huddled like a frightened turtle. Charles could not watch any longer, so once the pounding of his heart and the dryness in his throat subsided he cried out, "It figures. You hit like a girl."

Buster whirled towards the insulting voice, but instead of seeing a prime target, Buster McHale saw a mirror! The moment shocked him to his senses. It was a combination of realizing what he was doing and how he was behaving, coupled with the look on the face of Charles. The Hayes boy was looking at him with an expression of disgust that seared McHale's soul. It was like Charles' look was saying, 'do you see now what a loser you really are'? What Buster McHale saw in the mirror of his soul was really, really ugly. In fact, within his young seventeen year old spirit, he saw a beast. Disgusted with himself, he quickly threw on his clothes, brushed past Charles Hayes, and ran out of the locker room.

Charles moved towards Myles. Luckily, or so it seemed at the time, there was no gym class planned for next period.

"Myles?" There was no response from the pile on the floor.

"Myles, listen to me." Nothing.

"People like Buster have serious issues. Think about it. Buster McHale has probably got such a low self-image, that he has to pick on us weaker guys to feel better about himself." Charles was encouraged by his new train of thought, even though Myles still did not show that was listening. "Sure, physically he's bigger and stronger than us, but mentally, where it really counts in life; we have the advantage. He's a bully because he's scared. He pushes us around, because he needs to lash out in anger at a world that's hurt him in some way. All the bullies are the same, Myles. Did you see how the big coward ran out of here when I told him he hit like a girl? He's bigger than us, but he's not tougher!

You and I possess that kind of inner strength that will one day move mountains. My Pastor talks about it all the time. I believe him. I even think there's a verse in the Bible that says, 'the meek shall inherit the earth'. That's us, Myles! Physically, and I suppose socially too, we are the meek. The bullies may hate us, but the time will come when we, the weak, the tormented, the victims, will push back."

The late bell rang.

"Listen," Charles continued, torn between remaining with his burdened friend and getting his report and returning to social studies class. "I've got to get back. I'll meet you during lunch later, and we'll keep talking about it." He paused for a long moment. "Okay?"

"Myles, do you hear me? I will meet you…"

Suddenly Myles responded for the first time since his friend Charles entered the locker room.

"I'm fine, Charles. I'll be alright. Just go. I'll be fine."

Then he nervously added, "Please don't tell anyone I'm here. I don't want anyone to know about this."

Myles Langston continued to sob silently. Charles didn't know what to do next: leave or stay? He chose to do the latter.

It was a decision he would end up regretting for many years to come.

Meanwhile, Buster walked directly from the gym to the parking lot. He got into his car and started to drive away from the school. He had no particular destination in mind, but he felt like something was very wrong with him, and he knew that he had to get away to figure it out.

He drove to Riverton Park, and sat underneath a pavilion, secluded and sheltered from the light drizzle of rain. Slumped on a picnic bench, he stared at the cement floor. The same question continuously circled his mind. *What is the matter with me?*

Buster knew that he was gifted athletically. He starred in football, basketball and baseball, and he had always thought that being the best was really cool. He realized that at some point it had gone to his head. Just being the best eventually wasn't good enough. He had developed a need to show others just how much better than everybody else he was, and the easiest way to do this was to show those who were weaker than him what miserable failures they really were.

He searched for some ulterior reason for the way he acted. He looked for someone else to blame, but he knew there was no one to find but himself. *I am not a bully because somebody hurt me. I am not mean, disrespectful, and overly rough because that is way that I was brought up. No! No! No! Nobody did anything wrong to make me this way, and no one is responsible for my boorish behavior but me! What is the matter with me?*

The image of the utterly defeated little Myles Langston would give his mind no rest. *Slap!* He had cracked the poor, pitifully defenseless little guy right across his face.

Why would I do that? Do I have some pent-up aggressions that I need to get out of my system? I play football and hit people all the time. I do get my aggressions out. What is the matter with me?

As he sat at the picnic table, not knowing just what to do with himself, Buster made a decision. He was going to change! *No more bullying, terrorizing, teasing, and harassment! I am done.*

Right where he sat Buster lurched forward and threw up.

Later that night, two very separate, yet deeply connected events took place almost simultaneously. While Pastor Ronald Langston sat in his den preparing Sunday's sermon, his son Myles was upstairs sneaking into his father's gun chest. Myles had watched his Dad once hide the key under the lamp in his parent's bedroom. The memory of the key's location was emblazed in his mind just in case he ever went through with something he'd considered many times before. Myles methodically removed a revolver and some bullets. Hurrying to his own room, he caught a glimpse of his mother as she left the bathroom. He wanted to say something, but decided it would be better to just get on with it. Myles Langston did not have love for anyone tonight.

At the very same moment in time, both Myles Langston and Buster McHale sat alone in their respective bedrooms. Both young men were feeling deeply troubled, and both were staring at their phones.

Myles was considering calling Charles Hayes. He remembered that Charles had tried to talk to him during lunch. He did not call.

Buster McHale made the decision to pick up his phone. He'd experienced a personal epiphany today, and the guilt he felt was overwhelming. He had to talk to someone about it, and he chose none other than one of his chief antagonists: Mr. Moss.

The phone rang.

"Hello?"

"Mr. Moss? This is Buster McHale."

Buster McHale? A part of Brendan was in awe, but he still managed to encourage the youth to speak. "Go ahead Buster; what can I do for you?"

Buster told Mr. Moss all about what had happened in the boys' locker room. He went into detail, even though it was painful to describe his actions. Brendan listened in a near state of shock. He had heard confession before, but never would he have expected to hear one from Buster McHale. Brendan knew kids well. He easily recognized that this kid was hurting. The self-loathing was impossible to overlook. This confession was real, and it was raw. Brendan thought, *this kid will never be the same again, and that will be good for everyone.*

"I hate myself, Mr. Moss. When I saw what a monster I was and realized how terribly I treated kids like Myles, I got sick to my stomach. I want to stop this. There's no reason for me to act like this and I want to do something about it. I called you because I figured you might have some suggestions. When I saw myself in the mirror today and then saw the way Myles was sitting there all crumbled to the ground, I recognized something sinister and evil about my behavior. I need help. Can you help me, Mr. Moss?"

This was surreal. Brendan could barely accept that this confession of guilt was coming from none other than Riverton's biggest bully, Buster

McHale. "You'll get through this, Buster. I think that you are beginning to see that Myles Langston is a human being, a person with feelings and pain, and yes, you have been an instrument in his hurt. But here's what I've always believed: Each one of us is capable of changing the way we live, act, and behave at any moment we choose to. I'm sensing that you are at that point."

"So what do I do now?" Buster finished.

Mr. Moss sighed. "Here's what I would do. Look for Myles tomorrow at school," Brendan suggested. "Hopefully he'll be with Charles, so there will be less apprehension on his part when you approach him. Then," Brendan stated decisively, "share your heart, Buster. Apologize. Tell him how wrong you were, and then ask him for forgiveness. Myles is a good kid. Kids bully him because of how he looks and acts, and I suppose that oddity scares them a bit. I don't really understand it, although I wish I did." Brendan paused. "Maybe then I could put a stop to it. Anyway Buster, coming forward like this is a big step towards reconciliation. I heard about what happened today before you even told me. I don't want to sugar-coat things. From what I've heard, Myles took it hard. I think anyone would. Talk to him, try to get to know him, and I believe that he will accept your sincere apology. In fact," Brendan urged confidently, "you could be a leader. The kids look up to you. If they hear you say that bullying is wrong, then perhaps they'll follow your lead, and we can put an end to this bullying nonsense at Riverton."

Buster thanked Mr. Moss for his advice and guidance. He was impressed with how cordially the man had received him. He didn't deserve to have anyone be nice to him, let alone a teacher whom he'd repeatedly disrespected and challenged. Buster was glad he called. Apologizing tomorrow would be uncomfortable, but he would do it. Having the opportunity to fix things was, in fact, thrilling.

The Langston house was quiet but for the drone of the television set downstairs. His mother and father were watching the TV evangelist, Joyce Meyers. Twenty or so minutes earlier, Myles' Mom invited him to join them.

"Joyce is going to talk about dealing with depression and being different in a world that is often cruel and uncaring."

He answered, "not tonight."

Why would he listen to that? He was a living, breathing expert on the topic.

But not much longer.

A couple of years back his father took Myles on a hunting trip. He showed his son how to load a pistol and other types of firearms.

All he needed tonight was a pistol.

But first there was the note.

Myles figured that the least he could do was leave some sort of explanation behind. He felt he owed his parents that much. So he secured a single piece of paper on the clipboard he always kept on the side of his bed. Myles wrote his final letter of love.

"Mom and Dad,

I know that what I'm about to do is going to break your hearts and I wish there was some other way to put an end to this life of mine. But there isn't. You see a future for me. You see me graduating college and making lots of money and somehow, Dad, you envision that I will serve the Lord with my life. Only that's your life, Dad, not mine. There's not going to be a great job or a happy life for me. There's not going to be a wife and grandchildren. I am not someone who will ever live out the American dream. I don't see what you two see. All I see is pain. I hate everything about who and what I am. I can't do this anymore. Inside my head, I am a normal person. My thoughts are like everybody else's. It's my physicality that has destroyed me. Look at me. I'm ugly, scrawny, weak, and everyone finds me repulsive. People hate me just because of the way I look. Kids at school tease me, call me names, question my sexuality, and generally go out of their way to make my life miserable. I can't take it anymore. All I ever really wanted was to be accepted, liked, appreciated for what I have to offer, and to be someone's friend. I did have Charles. Make sure you show Charles this note and tell him I said thank you. I thank him for seeing the real me and enjoying what he saw. Don't forget to thank Charles for me. And thank you too. I had the best parents. I saw in your eyes the pain you both endured because of me. It tore at my heart when I saw the grief you both went through because I was your son. I know that I shamed and embarrassed you. I didn't want to do that. I wish I hadn't. You both came to my aid and helped me through the horrible days of my life. I love you so much. Please forgive me.

Myles.

P.S. Dad: I do believe that Jesus died for my sins. And I believe that once I've completed this deed, He will be there waiting for me. You taught me well. I just can't do this anymore."

Myles dropped the pen to the floor. It was a note he had imagined writing numerous times throughout the years. While he would sit during the car ride home from school with his mother, he would think of the words to say. He hoped that whatever he wrote would be well said and insightful. Today he had no feelings about how he worded his final note to his parents. After a moment Myles' eyes shifted from the pen on the floor to the revolver on his bed. This part too was something he had pictured in his mind many times before. He wondered: Is this going to hurt? Myles never liked physical pain of any kind. Even a bee sting scared him. He suddenly remembered a time when he was sitting out on his swing set while a bumble bee hovered around his head. He screamed for his mother to come out and rescue him. Mom ran to his aid as she always did. Mom and Dad were terrific parents. They were always there for him. But all he ever did was embarrass and disappoint them. Myles was certain that his parents were ashamed of what he was. Which was what? What was he exactly that was so awful that the other kids hated him so much?

Myles lifted the gun and placed it against the side of his head. Tears began to fall as he thought about why he had to do this. I just wanted to be normal. I wanted other kids to like me. I hoped to make my parents proud.

Myles Langston loved his mother and father.

But he had no love for anyone tonight.

He had a job to do.

Two hours later, Brendan's phone rang again.

The voice on the other end of the line was frantic. It was Charles Hayes.

"Slow down Charles," Brendan pronounced gravely, explaining to the kid that he hadn't understood a word of what he was trying to tell him. "Who are you talking about?"

"Myles Langston!" Charles sobbed pitifully. "He's dead, Mr. Moss. I went to go see him, and he is dead. He shot himself in the head!"

The words came through all too clearly at last. After soothing Charles, he hung up and dropped his chin to his chest.

Suicide. Why did he ever want to be a school teacher? Why did he have to care so much for these kids?

The next morning the school hallways were buzzing with the tragic news. Counselors were busy trying to explain life and death to kids who were mostly too distraught to hear. Rumors were flying about why the fourteen year old would do such a stupid thing. Much of the gossip was the same.

The story of the Langston suicide and Buster McHale's involvement rippled through the Riverton School District. No one knew about the epilogue except for Mr. Moss and Buster. The metamorphosis of Buster McHale came too late to save the life of Myles Langston.

The funeral was set for Saturday morning. The wake on the preceding Friday night attracted one of the biggest crowds in the history of Riverton. Families who weren't even familiar with the Langston family came to pay their respects.

People swarmed. They were angry. Parents who sent their children to the Riverton School District had had enough. They were tired of hearing about all of the bullying and harassment that some kids were forced to endure. They were tired of learning about how administration refused to step in and stop it. The talk was that teachers were turning their heads, while kids were being brutalized by their peers. It was as if the people's mourning was a collective voice crying out: "Stop this"!

School superintendent, Bailey Thompson was inundated with a steady stream of phone calls from irate community members. The demands were similar. What is going on over there? Can I trust my child to be safely protected from harm? How could this have ever happened? A spirit of revenge simmered in the hearts of many of the attending community members, and the name Buster McHale rolled from tongue to tongue.

The Saturday morning service was held at the Riverton Methodist Church. Pastor Ronald Langston and his wife Rae needed to be helped to their seats. The service was packed. There were hymns and scripture readings, and a poignant sermon was delivered by a pastor from a neighboring church.

Brendan sat on the left side of the church, near the back. He had arrived early to find a seat. He watched the Langston family as they were escorted down the aisle and his heart broke for them. *This morning they would be the chief mourners. It was their turn today. Everybody gets a turn at some time. Today it was theirs.*

He'd been there. Five years ago he was the chief mourner. He too knew and had experienced loss, and yet, this was different. This cut right through the fabric of existence. This was pain beyond endurance. Myles was so young.

When he couldn't stand to look at the grieving parents a second longer, Brendan turned his head to survey the crowd. He noticed that Bailey Thompson and a large number of other faculty members were in attendance. High school and middle school kids were scattered throughout the church. It was a good sign to see so many young people present. Perhaps it was a sign of hope.

His eyes locked on a young face standing against the back wall. The boy's massive presence loomed largely above others beside him. Buster McHale returned his stare. Even from a distance, Brendan could see that his eyes were bloodshot. *Will there be another suicide here in Riverton?*

Brendan knew that he would never forget the phone call he had received from Buster the night of the Langston suicide. The confession and the heart rendering plea for forgiveness came before anyone knew. The McHale boy had wanted to make amends, and Brendan was positive that Buster would have followed through with his sincere intentions. Myles hadn't given him the chance. *He must know what people will accuse him of. What could the poor, broken soul be thinking showing up at the funeral? He must blame himself, and let's face it; the blame is right where it belongs.*

Tears flowed unabashedly from his cheeks as Brendan watched Pastor and Mrs. Langston follow the pallbearers out of the church. The face of the youngest pallbearer, Charles Hayes was almost unrecognizable. The vivacity that usually emboldened the boy had abandoned him today.

As Brendan rose to his feet, a deep ache clutched at both his legs. He wasn't injured. No, the pain he felt was the emotional weeding its way into the physical. He wished that it was just an injury he felt and not his heart breaking for the Langston family. An injured leg would eventually heal with rest and rehabilitation. Brendan would have welcomed a physical ache over what he had right now. Body parts heal. Ailing tissues can be replaced by new, vibrant healthy tissues.

Nothing could replace the loss of a child.

And nothing could soothe the hurt of just how the young man left this earth. Suicide. Myles Langston wasn't the first and he certainly wouldn't be the last. But how does one stop it? He was a teacher. He deals with these hurting kids every day. What could he have done or said to brighten this particular child's disposition and made the boy choose otherwise? What power if any did he fail to utilize? Why didn't he see the symptoms earlier and come to the kid's aid? Why, why, why?

And then the biggest 'why' of all hit him in the gut.

Why didn't I call Myles once I knew what happened in the locker room?

Charles had told me all about Myles, Buster slapping his face and all I had to do was take five minutes to talk to the boy. He liked me and I know he would have listened to me. I don't know what I could have said to prevent this tragedy, but at least I could have tried! I'm a teacher. That's what we do. We deal with kids' depressions, anxieties, and we attempt to lead them back to safety. I knew all about it. What did I do instead?

Brendan remembered.

Jonathan's soccer team had a game. I went and on the way home I stopped at the Mall. Later that night Buster phoned me. Awhile after that came the horrible news from Charles. There was time in between the calls. I had time to do something.

But I didn't.

People followed the procession out of the church and began to congregate in clusters on the front lawn. Brendan politely brushed by those who wished to engage him in conversation. He was on a mission. He was desperately hoping to locate the McHale boy. He found him standing alone at the bottom of the cement stairs that led up to the church. He looked like he was waiting. He was. He was waiting for Mr. Moss.

Once Brendan spotted Buster, he immediately headed in his direction. He had no idea what he would say, but his spirit told him that he needed to come up with something. The boy needed him. For reasons known only to Buster, Brendan was the adult the kid reached out to during his darkest hour, and now his situation must appear even darker.

Just before Brendan reached Buster McHale, Mrs. Rae Langston rushed up to the youth. Her verbal assault startled everyone nearby. "Did you even know him?" Mrs. Rae Langston cried hysterically. "Did you know my son loved birds? He would draw pictures of them and sometimes frame them. There are some on the walls of his room. Did you know that Myles' dream was to be an air-traffic controller? He loved birds and planes."

Her husband grabbed her by her shoulders, and a resonant scream of pain escaped from her mouth.

"Your mother," she spat, "She's proud of you, isn't she? I was proud of Myles! My son was a good boy, with a good heart, and we had plans! He would come home crying from school, and I would have to invent some game to cheer him up. Who do I play with now? What do I do with the clarinet that's on the floor beside his bed? He yelled at me because I moved it while cleaning his room. Now I'm afraid to touch it. Did you know that?"

Overwhelmed by the onslaught, Buster McHale collapsed to the ground. There was a loud crack as he fell forward. His head struck the pavement. No one moved to help him until Brendan Moss came forward. There was blood on the sidewalk.

"Call 911!" Brendan shouted to no one in particular. "Somebody help me turn him over."

Two men jumped in to assist, turning Buster over onto his back. Brendan put his ear to the kid's chest to see if he was still breathing. He was. Someone handed Brendan a towel. He firmly applied it to Buster's head and found to his relief that the damage was minimal.

Less than five minutes later, an ambulance was on the scene. While the trained medical personnel carefully lifted Buster McHale into the ambulance, the youngster began to regain consciousness. It was a good sign.

As the ambulance drove away, Brendan checked his cell phone for the number Buster had called him from earlier in the week. Once he found it, he tapped in the digits and sighed in relief as Mrs. McHale picked up the line. He told her what had just occurred and reassured her that her son was in good hands and that the kid would be alright.

"You should have seen him, Mrs. McHale. Buster is in a great deal of emotional pain right now, and I'm sure he blames himself for the Langston suicide." Over the phone he could hear the mother catch her breath and try to suppress a moan. "But you would have been proud of him. He stood there and took the criticism and insinuations like a man. No," Brendan quickly corrected, "not many men would have shown the strength of character that your boy did. He's probably got a tough road ahead of him, but this is no longer the same Buster McHale we all grew to hate. I've never before witnessed such courage under fire, and I will never forget it."

Later that same Saturday afternoon, Brendan arrived home to an empty house. The house was often empty these days. As he sat on the edge of his couch, Brendan's thoughts returned to Myles Langston. Myles was brought up in the church. His father was a pastor. Brendan wondered: Did Myles Langston believe in the God of the Bible? Did the poor unhappy child believe in any God at all? Brendan reflected on what he knew and had seen about how the kid was treated by peers. Did Myles ever wonder: Where is God when I need him?

"Be there to meet the kid, sweetheart." He whispered aloud, speaking again to his deceased wife. "Myles will love it there. The Bible says there's no pain, no heartache, no sorrow, and that there's only joy. He had it tough down here." A lump formed in his throat. "Sometimes I hate it here too. If it weren't for our three kids, I'd gladly remove myself from this hell-hole and join you up there. I really would. But I'm still here, still in good health, and still missing you terribly. I love you, sweetheart, and I always will. There will never be anyone else for me."

Chapter 6

He didn't even know why he was there.

Brendan was sitting on a chair outside a circle of medical staff who were attending to Abby Richardson, a former student of his. The sixteen year old had phoned Mr. Moss in the middle of the night complaining of severe labor pains and asking for a ride to the hospital.

"Sure, I'll take you," Brendan assured her, "but why are you asking me? Where are your parents or where," he said out loud what he was thinking, "is the baby's father?"

"Darrin left last week," she stated matter-of-factly, "and I couldn't get a hold of my Mom. She got mad at me for taking something of hers and now she's probably at the bar doing what she always does."

Brendan was aware that Abby's mother was an alcoholic.

"I tried calling a few other people, but no one was able to take me. Some of my friends are working, and my grandma won't answer the phone. I know you live a half-hour away, but I need somebody I can count on. You've always been there for me, Mr. Moss. When I told you I was pregnant, I knew you were disappointed in me, but you never stopped liking me. That meant a lot and I never forgot it."

Now almost six hours later, Brendan sat in the delivery room as though he were the expectant father. A sixteen year old mother from Riverton High was not out of the ordinary. It happened all the time. So many adolescents were having unprotected sex, and some even began their sexual experimentation as early as the 7th grade. It was sad.

It irked Brendan that the baby's biological father had left town. *They want to play, but they don't want to pay. My goodness, if the two of them had only waited until they were older and ready for the role of parenthood, how much more would they have enjoyed one of the best experiences in life!*

Like the way he and Emily had.

"I'm just telling you what they taught us in Lamaze class," Brendan had found himself apologizing, as Emily scolded him when he told her to breathe.

"You tell me to breathe one more time, and I swear I'll sock you in the jaw!" she had smiled. It was not a joyful smile.

At 1:21 AM on Friday morning, October the second, Amanda Moss made her first appearance. Brendan didn't know what to expect. She was wet, red, slimy, and absolutely beautiful! He instantly fell in love with her. She was theirs!

A few hours later, as the new parents sat alone in the hospital room, Brendan reached for his wife's hand and squeezed it tightly.

"I've got to tell you something," he spoke softly. "I've never seen anything like that in my life."

"Hey!" Emily said back. "I've never seen a baby being born either."

"That's not what I meant."

Brendan had been thirty-six years old the day he became a father for the first time. Though a recent graduate of his Lamaze class, he was no more prepared for what he'd witnessed than any other first time father. It was miraculous!

"I'm talking about you," he smiled at his wife. "I just watched you go through an incredible ordeal. I don't think I've ever been more proud of you. Your strength, your endurance, your will to see this thing through, was the greatest act of courage I've ever witnessed."

"There was no way out of it, you know."

"I know that," he responded to her playful tease, "but I just cannot be blasé about what I watched you do for us. We have a daughter! My God, you did it sweetheart. I was no help and you didn't even need my help. Man," he had smiled broadly and wiped a tear from his cheek, "I will never forget this day."

Abby Richardson was still too young to be the trooper his Emily had been years ago. His wife had delivered three healthy babies through natural child birth. Emily had not taken any drugs, had no spinals, and had let her water break when it was good and ready to on its own. "You are my natural woman," he whispered to her after their third, Jonathan, was born.

Abby Richardson's young body and young mind was not really ready for childbirth. Oh, the baby came out healthy and strong, but emotionally, a sixteen year old is not as fit as a woman in her twenties. There are always exceptions of course, but Brendan held to his theory, kids were not meant to be having kids, and he wished that he had the power to make these young pregnant Riverton girls understand that.

Abby Richardson went through a horrendous ordeal. The doctor induced her and later decided that a Cesarean delivery was her best option. That was major surgery, and she was facing it without the support of her family. Brendan could see that she was in terrible pain, and the only hand she had to hold was that of her former middle school math teacher, a man she trusted, but had no real relationship with.

Abby named her newborn daughter, Sara. When it was all over and done with, the girl appeared happy, though exhausted. She seemed relieved that it was all over, although for Abby, her trials as a young single mother were only just beginning.

On the drive home, Brendan started to think about Buster McHale. It had been days since the funeral, and he hadn't heard a thing about the boy. The Riverton football team had lost their game on Saturday night, but had still qualified for the sectional playoffs. The rumor was that Buster hadn't shown up for Saturday's game, and that this was the primary reason for the loss.

Jonathan had a playoff game of his own tonight. The soccer sectionals were always fun for Brendan, but this year his enthusiasm was tempered by the knowledge that since Jon was a senior, any sectional game might be Jon's last.

"I'm on my way to the school," Jon shouted as he hurried down the stairs. "The bus is leaving at 4:30."

"Play hard," Brendan encouraged. It was the same phrase he intoned before every athletic event.

It was already four o'clock, and the game was scheduled to be played under the lights at 7:30. The Ashton boys were the third seed and would be going up against top-seeded International Prep. It would require a huge upset for Ashton to win, but as they say, you never know!

Brendan glanced at the clock. He still had plenty of time to go to the YMCA to lift weights and run on the treadmill. There was no need for him to shower. It was important that he was at this game on time.

It was four o'clock.

The New York State Commissioner of Education, Robert Haines, glanced at the clock. The impromptu meeting with the governor and a handful of congressmen was about to begin. The Governor of New York, Raleigh McDevitt, was a republican from Rochester. He was near to completing his first term as governor and was up for reelection in November. McDevitt was a man who supported big business. There were three things he hated: welfare, democrats, and unions. He had an especially strong dislike of the state teachers' union.

"We don't live in the same world we used to. There may have been a time when a teacher's right to tenure was a sound principal, but in our present economy, tenure is a dangerous and impractical convention. It's not right! Our teachers do not have any measure of accountability. Look at our children. Many cannot read well and struggle with basic mathematics. As a nation, our children are so far behind in their comprehension of the sciences that it's embarrassing. The rest of the world is passing us by, and I'll tell you why."

Everyone present was listening.

"Do you think China provides tenure for their teachers?" The governor continued. "If students aren't succeeding, teachers are fired! You either get the job done, or you are out on your tail. Isn't that the way it is in business?

In government, if the voters are displeased with your performance, they choose someone else to take your place," McDevitt paused, "and that's how it should be!"

"Excuse me Governor," a reporter interrupted, "but it's hardly fair to compare our educational system to China. At a certain level they only continue to educate the best. We try to give everybody a fair shot. Our system is called 'No Child Left Behind'. I believe a lot of young people get left behind in China and are designated to other fields of labor. A child here in the United States has the freedom to chart their own course in life. Now it may be true that many of them snub this opportunity but at least the chance is there. From what I've heard and read the kids in China live for the government. In America, the government exists for the kids."

Heads were nodding in agreement.

State Senator, William Quigley from New York City, raised his hand. "Governor McDevitt," he began, "the state teachers union is probably the strongest and largest union in New York. Are you proposing that we would be able to win a fight against them? This tenure issue is the biggest egg in their basket. How do we steal their prized jewel?"

Governor Raleigh McDevitt leaned back in his chair. "How do we do it, Senator Quigley? We take them on one case at a time. We set a precedent. Once a single case has been won, we create more."

"So, how soon does this process begin?"

"I have a friend, who has recently become the superintendent in a town called Riverton. It's a small district in Western New York. My associate has already chosen our first victim." A group of them laughed at the terminology. "There will be others we will target. It shouldn't be too long now. Mr. Haines?" the governor motioned towards the Commissioner of Education, "Do you have a recent update?"

Robert Haines cleared his throat. *Yes, he did have a recent update on the plan underway in Riverton, but no, he didn't like it one bit.* There was something dirty about the whole thing Perhaps it was that what was once theoretical now affected a particular man. He couldn't put his finger on it, but it gave him the chills. Maybe it was because his daughter had decided to go into teaching. This was going to be a big mess, and not easy as everybody surrounding him seemed to think.

Haines answered in a monotone. "The administration is searching for more influential accusations to levy against Mr. Moss. We hope to remove this man's tenure by the spring."

The remainder of the meeting revolved around finances. School districts throughout the state were struggling to come up with the means to remain within their budgets. The projections and predictions of how many staff members districts would be able to afford were despairingly low. People would be losing their jobs, lots of people.

As the men and women who attended the meeting went their separate ways, Robert Haines overheard two state congressmen speaking in the hall.

"What the hell happened?" an older man was asking a state representative half his age. "When I was a kid there were plenty of good teachers, and solid athletic and music programs. I don't remember money ever being a problem. What happened?"

The younger man shook his head, "The government wasn't involved back then. Schools didn't rely on 'big brother' to fund them. Communities ran their own school districts. There were no expensive state exams or mandates that change with the wind."

The older man grabbed the young representative's arm, and shook his finger in his face.

"We're not the bad guys. The public school system needs us."

The younger man smiled.

"They did fine without us back then."

After a thirty minute jog on the treadmill, Brendan wiped his face with a towel, and proceeded with his weight training for the day. He liked to work out with both free weights and the nautilus. As he headed towards the free weight section for the third time, Brendan immediately recognized a well-built young man preparing the bench press unit with a hefty amount of weights. It was Buster McHale.

Brendan's mind was reeling. He hadn't seen or heard of Buster McHale in weeks. The boy wasn't attending school and there were rumors that he had left town. Moss overheard more than one person express their distain and judgment over the poor kid. Brendan had made a few efforts to seek him out but at each turn his attempts to find the young man were stymied. He did find out that Buster was supposedly still living at home with his parents, but that a tutor was being provided by the school district until the kid decided to return. That was a while ago. Brendan really hadn't checked on the whereabouts of Buster McHale since and as far as he knew the former star athlete had fallen off the face of the earth. Yet throughout that period of time Brendan never stopped thinking about the phone call that night. This big kid he was now staring at was no longer the bully of Riverton. This was somebody else.

And Mr. Moss was about to meet him.

"Hi, Mr. Moss," Buster held out his hand. "I knew you still worked out. I was hoping to run into you." For a long moment there was an uncomfortable silence. "Do you mind if we take a break so we can talk?"

Brendan glanced at the clock. Jon's game wasn't too far away, but Buster seemed earnest. He remembered the late night phone call and answered, "Sure, Buster."

They walked away from the weight area and over towards a section where people could remove their shoes, coats, and athletic wear. There were chairs next to a wooden bin, where they sat down. "I always noticed that you kept a Bible on your desk at school. A couple of times I saw you reading it," Buster sighed. "At the time I just thought you were a loser, or some kind of religious freak. Myles," his voice cracked at the mention of the deceased boy's name, "came up to your desk once and the two of you starting talking. It was about Jesus and going to Heaven. I listened, even though I hated both of you." A large lump formed in the youngster's throat. "Is Myles in Heaven?"

Buster's eyes began to glisten with tears. Brendan reached over and placed an arm over Buster's shoulder.

"Is he?" Buster wanted to know.

"Myles Langston was raised in a Christian home," Brendan began. "No one can ever really know another person's heart, but I do believe that Myles believed that Jesus was his Lord and Savior. So if you are asking me," he paused, "and you are; I would answer yes. Myles Langston is now in Heaven."

What else was he supposed to say? Myles took his own life and that is a terribly wrong thing to do. But who was he, Brendan Moss, to judge the poor kid?

"People have all kinds of issues. You are not the only one on this earth responsible for bad things. Here's the way I understand it. Myles Langston, because of his faith in Jesus Christ, is now alive and well, up in Heaven. The Bible says that in Heaven there is no pain, no tears, no heat, and no sorrow." Brendan could immediately tell that that perked Buster up a bit. The kid liked the sound of that.

"So is Myles good now?"

My God, there was so much that Brendan Moss really didn't know! He knew what he would have to say to ease the kid's guilt, but what if he was wrong?

No, his spirit scolded him. You are not wrong! Tell him everything you know.

"Like I said, Buster, we've all got issues. Every one of us has done things we regret and are ashamed of, but when we trust that God sent Jesus to save us, we are totally and completely forgiven."

That last statement got Buster's attention. As he stared down at the floor, he asked hopefully, "Does God forgive anything?"

"God will forgive you, Buster. All you got to do is ask."

"Thanks, Mr. Moss."

Brendan cut a few repetitions out of his workout and managed to get to the game five minutes before the scheduled start. He watched what turned out to be an exciting game, but the Ashton boys lost the tightly, well-played match, 1-0. International Prep, a high school made up of foreign students who have played soccer since they could walk, scored the lone goal with four minutes remaining.

So that was that! Jonathan Moss would never play soccer in a league again. As the contest wound down to the final seconds, he watched his youngest walk off the field. Jon hadn't shaved his face in over a week. The baby of the family was beginning to look like a man. When did that happen?

On the drive back home, Brendan recalled two bittersweet memories. The first had occurred seven years ago after his oldest, Amanda, played her last sectional soccer game. As the seconds had wound down to zero, Brendan had squeezed his wife's hand and hugged her close. Emily felt strong and healthy. "Soccer was a season in her life. You and I are forever!"

His second memory was more bitter. His older son, Matthew, had been the starting point guard for Ashton High's basketball team. In a semi-final playoff game against heavily favored Randolph High, the Ashton boys had only trailed by five points with less than a minute to go. Matthew had attempted a three-pointer from the corner and missed.

Season over! He would never have the pleasure of seeing Matt play varsity basketball again. This time as Brendan had lamented the end, he had sat alone in the stands. Emily was not beside him. Brendan did not have her hand to squeeze or have her ear to whisper in to.

"You and I are forever" was replaced by a phrase he had uttered to himself for the first time that night, and had repeated often many times since: "What am I going to do without you?" He needed his wife's gentle understanding and sound advice. He needed her to help him make decisions. What was the purpose of living without her? What was his purpose? He would live, work, play, enjoy his children; and he would find out.

Chapter 7

It was two days before Christmas and almost all of Brendan's shopping was done. He was at the Bon-Ton looking at outfits for newborns. He figured since Abby Richardson didn't have a lot of family to help her out that he should purchase something for Sara for Christmas. He chose a Buffalo Bills uniform sized for nine-month-old. Why not? Little girls don't always have to wear pink, do they? He bought Abby something too. While he stood in line he recalled the first pint sized Buffalo Bills jersey he ever purchased.

"Here," Emily had whispered so as not to be heard by their three sleeping children, "wheel them over this way."

Brendan had lightly pushed two bicycles designed to look like motorcycles towards the tree. The tree was filled with special bulbs designed by the children over the past few days. Each year the total of bulbs grew.

"Give me that too," she pointed to a box with a sticker marked: Jonathan.

Later that morning, Emily gave the box to their five-year-old, and encouraged him to open it. Jon grabbed the present and tore the wrapping from it. It was a Buffalo Bills uniform! Inside the box was a blue jersey, white pants, and a red helmet with the team insignia on the side. Across the back of the jersey the name read: Moss. It was hard to guess just who was more excited: Jon or his father!

For the remainder of Christmas morning, the Moss family was very busy. Emily Moss was in the kitchen preparing a late afternoon turkey dinner, while Amanda and Matthew Moss were riding their brand new motorcycle bikes all over the downstairs. Jonathan Moss was dressed in his new football gear playing tackle football with Brendan in the living room.

After dinner the three children had gone to the playroom, and he and Emily were left alone at the dining room table. "I have everything a man could want," he said to his wife. "I've got an amazing woman, three healthy kids, and so much more to look forward to."

"What do you look forward to the most?"

Brendan grew thoughtful.

"Someday these three," he referred to the children, "are going to be gone, and then it's just going to be you and me. We are going to travel all over the world and have the time of our lives!"

Emily grabbed her husband's face between her hands and drew him to her.

They had kissed.

"I can't wait!" She had breathed excitedly.

Holding this latest rendition in his hands, Brendan was forced to look away from the gift for just a second.

"My God," he whispered aloud, not even caring if a shopper overheard, "I miss you so much!"

When he got home he found a note on the table from Jon, informing him that he was going to spend the night at his buddy Zach's house. Matt was out working for the night, so Brendan opened up his laptop computer to check his e-mail. While he was reading a message from his brother, an advertisement popped up on the screen. It was from Holland America for a one week cruise to Bermuda on a ship called the Veendam.

He and Emily had made reservations five years ago for the very same trip. It was only Christmas time, but his wife was so excited that she booked the trip six months in advance. Brendan's brother John was going to drop them off in New York City on Sunday morning, July 1st, 2006.

Emily Moss had passed away on January 30th, 2006.

At school the next day, Brendan stood at the art room door conversing with Mr. Hamlin, the middle school art teacher. They were talking about Mr. Hamlin's vacation home in Florida.

"Mr. Moss!" He turned to locate the loud voice. "There's a fight!"

Sure enough, a seventh grader and an eighth grader were going at it. Both boys were wildly throwing fists. The eight grade English teacher, Maya Gregg, was the first to arrive on the scene. She grabbed one of the boys, and pulled him away from the fracas. Brendan moved in with his arms up to block the hits of the other boy, Oscar Campenelli.

Brendan noticed two other boys filming the fight on their cell phones. The trend was to film a fight, put it on the internet, and watch it later with some friends. Sick to say the least!

No sooner had Mr. Moss thought that things were about to settle down, than Oscar Campenelli lunged forward to resume his attack. Brendan reacted. He put up his hands to stop Oscar. The seventh grader pushed Mr. Moss roughly aside, causing Brendan to fall back against the water fountain.

The moment Oscar Campenelli freed himself from faculty obstruction; he leaped towards the other boy. Ms. Gregg, all one-hundred and ten pounds of her, was no match for the violent onslaught. Neither was the surprised eighth grader. Oscar pummeled the frightened youth with a barrage of punches which mostly hit their mark. One caught the boy square in the face, breaking his nose.

Mr. Moss reacted again. He grabbed Oscar from behind and drove him to the floor. It took every bit of strength Brendan had in his sixty-year-old body to hold the kid there. As he firmly leaned his weight down on the boy, Brendan noticed some blood on the floor by Oscar's face.

Uh-oh. That wasn't good.

Suddenly, Brendan found Tyler Haden kneeling by his side. Other staff members had begun to gather in the hallways. Brendan let go of Oscar, got to his feet, and allowed himself to be led aside. As the faculty who were trained to deal with violent situations turned the kid over, Brendan quickly looked to see just how much blood there was. With a sigh of relief, he saw that any injury his intervention may have caused was miniscule.

The trained staff led Oscar Campenelli to the main office, while the other boy, Billy Weston, was taken to the nurse. They would both be sent home for the day, but they would be certain to return.

The next day, Mr. Moss was called in to a meeting with the principal. He sat at a table in the office and waited nearly five minutes. When Tyler Haden finally arrived, Brendan saw that the middle school principal was accompanied by Bailey Thompson, the school superintendent.

The two men joined Mr. Moss at the conference room table. There were no friendly greetings.

"Mr. Moss," the superintendent started, "yesterday you were responsible for injuring a child."

"Excuse me?"

Bailey Thompson looked over the papers he held in his hand. He turned to Mr. Haden.

"Could you please run the videotape, Tyler?"

The Riverton School District, had cameras installed in all the hallways. They were a helpful tool for identifying the perpetrators of violence, vandalism, or theft. Mr. Haden rewound the tape to the time of the fight between Oscar Campenelli and Billy Weston. The three men watched as the two boys mauled each other right underneath the camera located at the intersection of the perpendicular hallways.

They saw Maya Gregg enter the scene to separate the fighters. Next, Brendan Moss appeared.

They all saw Mr. Moss get violently shoved against the water fountain, and they observed Oscar Campenelli resume his physical assault. "I've seen enough." Mr. Thompson announced after Mr. Moss grabbed Oscar from behind and dropped him to the floor.

An eerie silence filled the room. "This is not the 1950s anymore, Mr. Moss," the superintendent began, "teachers in the Riverton School District will not physically punish young teenagers on my watch. Not only did you overstep your professional boundaries, but you injured the boy as well!"

Brendan sat speechless.

Tyler Haden was rummaging through his briefcase for a sheet of paper. He removed it and placed it down in front of Mr. Moss. "We need you to sign this, Brendan." There was a trace of nervousness in the principal's voice. Brendan immediately sensed that Haden was not 'into this', whatever 'this' was.

Brendan looked over the paper. Once again it was an official reprimand. Only this time, Brendan did not involve himself in an internal debate. This time he would not mentally weigh the pros and cons of signing. His mind was made up.

"I'm not signing this!" he refused, roughly pushed the sheet of paper towards the principal, where it lifted into the air and floated to the floor. Brendan pushed back his chair, stood, and turned to leave.

"Where do you think you're going?" Mr. Thompson asked.

"I'm a teacher, Mr. Thompson. I've got kids to teach!"

Once Brendan had gone, Bailey Thompson glanced over at Tyler Haden and grinned, "That went well."

Tyler Haden did not respond.

"Okay, what more do you have on the Richardson girl?"

"He was over there this past weekend, dropping off Christmas presents for the baby." That was all Tyler Haden knew.

"So, he drove her to the hospital to have the baby, and now he's bringing gifts."

Haden ignored the insinuation, but instead pursued a thought of his own.

"What does any of this have to do with revoking a teacher's tenure? This guy used to be a friend of mine. We taught math together for over ten years. He's not a criminal, Bailey. In fact, he's a very nice man, and in my opinion, an excellent math teacher and role model for the children of Riverton. You know as well as I do that if he hadn't acted swiftly, the Campenelli boy could have seriously injured Billy. He did his best to protect Billy, and Oscar's injuries are minor. As for implying that Brendan Moss is some kind of pedophile, well…"

"He's too old, and too expensive," Thompson interrupted. "Students need more freedom than Moss permits. Look at the discipline reports. He makes more work for you, the counselors, and your secretarial staff. Look Tyler," Thompson regressed to a softer tone, "I don't doubt that Brendan Moss was a fine instructor in his day. I am not criticizing his dedication and work ethic, but I am thinking that his time has passed. These kids need a softer touch, more understanding, and a pat on the back when they do behave. Moss is too tough. The future of education is changing. That's exactly the problem with tenure! Teachers get old, lose touch and cannot relate with the new generation, and there's not a thing administration can do about it. We're stuck with a slew of outdated, overpaid, old timers who have worn out their welcome. He's our test case," Thompson continued. "If we can show that guys like Moss shouldn't be allowed to remain on payroll because of tenure, than perhaps we can finally prove that this policy is archaic and should be done away with. Tenure is not a good thing for kids!"

Bailey Thompson excused himself, leaving Haden alone to think. Tyler Haden had lived in Riverton for his whole life. He had attended Catholic school through the eighth grade, but slid over to Riverton High as a freshman. The principal at the time had been William Golic.

Golic had been a big man, and the last person any Riverton student had wanted to face. Unlike the youth who currently stomped off to the office as though it were their God-given right, students in the sixties and seventies feared being sent to see Mr. Golic.

If Mr. Golic didn't like the way you spoke to an authority figure, he would give you a quick cuffing to the head. Few students, if any, made the same mistake twice. Young Tyler Haden was only sent to the office once during his years at Riverton High. He was talking to a girl in his history class and was told to stop.

"One more peep out of you, Tyler, and you're going to the office."

He couldn't resist, "Peep!"

His legs had begun to shake, as he was ordered out of the room and down to the office. He stood in front of the bench outside of the office door when Mr. Golic approached him.

"Why are you here?"

Tyler had never been so frightened in his life! All sorts of visions ran through his mind. What type of pain was this monster of a man going to inflict upon him? He prayed to God and whispered, "I'll never make a peep again!"

"Sit down," Mr. Golic had ordered, as he pointed towards the wooden bench.

Tyler sat. For fifteen of the most terrifying minutes of his life he sat still and waited for the principal to return with his punishment. He imagined just which side of his face would be struck and he grew especially concerned about how he knew Mr. Golic would phone his parents and how much trouble he would be in when he got home. *Why did I say peep?* Haden was never so scared in his entire life.

Mr. Golic returned.

"Come into my office, young man."

Tyler jumped to his feet.

"I won't do it again; I promise!" Tears began to flow down along his cheeks. "Please forgive me. I swear I'll never do anything bad again."

Tyler Haden would never forget how afraid he was that day.

Now forty years later, he was the principal, and no child was afraid of him.

Two weeks later, Brendan sat at his computer desk, writing before his first period. While his fingers tapped the keyboard, his door flung open. There in his doorway, stood Tyler Haden flanked on both sides by two police officers.

"You need to come with me, Mr. Moss."

It sounded so official.

"Take the things you need," Haden continued as though reciting a memorized verse, "and come with us, as we escort you out of the building."

What?

"Can you tell me what this is all about, Tyler?"

Brendan could tell that Haden felt extremely uncomfortable. "The Riverton School District," Haden pronounced, "is placing you on administrative leave. We have legitimate concerns about your conduct towards the students."

Brendan did not protest. He figured it was best to let Haden explain the charges against him. He wanted to hear it first. He would worry about a defense later.

"Administration and the Board of Education are presently looking into two separate matters. You and I have already spoken about the assault on

Oscar Campenelli. We are also investigating an incident of involvement with a female student."

"And just who is that?" Moss asked crisply, unable to take the sting out of his anger.

"I'm not allowed to discuss specifics," Haden sighed. "For now, I need you to gather your things and come with us."

Brendan could barely think straight. It was apparent that he was going to be escorted out of the school building by a pair of armed police officers, both of whom he was relatively familiar with. The officer on his left, Dexter Scaggs, had joined the Riverton Police Department twenty years ago. When officer Scaggs first moved to Western New York from New York City, he, his wife, and children were the first black family in town. Even though it was the late eighties, the Scaggs was still a little nervous about being the only blacks in an all white town. As Dexter and his brothers moved furniture into his new home, a delivery boy arrived with two large pepperoni pizzas, drinks, and a card. The card said, "Welcome to Riverton!", and it was signed by Brendan and Emily Moss.

The officer on his right was Ben Miller. Officer Miller was a lifelong resident of Riverton. He and his wife, Carol, only had one child, a boy named Damien. Damien Miller had had Mr. Moss for math when he was in the eighth grade.

One afternoon, as Damien was walking home from school, a gang of young thugs had stopped him on the street. One of the boys in the gang was upset, because Officer Miller had busted his older brother for selling drugs. He figured he would pay back Mr. Miller. He pulled out a box cutter and poked it against Damien's neck. A car suddenly pulled over near the boys, and a man got out. It was Mr. Moss.

"Need a ride home, Damien?" He asked as he pulled the child into his car. Once Damien was safely inside, Moss took a few steps towards the gang of boys. He was familiar with all of them.

"Don't think for a second that I still can't kick your ass!" He directed at the biggest boy with the box cutter.

"We're not in school now, Mr. Moss," one of the boys boldly shouted.

Moss smiled, "That's right. We're not."

Mr. Moss took Damien home and told his parents what happened. He gave the police the names of the boys who were present. Damien Miller never needed to be concerned for his safety again.

As the two officers and Principal Haden led him down the hallway, Brendan realized how embarrassed he was. Students just arriving at school, stood around in groups gawking. Brendan almost felt like smiling as he imagined their thoughts. *Was Mr. Moss a drug dealer? Did he murder somebody? Boy, when he got mad he sure looked like he could kill someone!* On his way out the door, Brendan exchanged glances with Dan Ross, the president of the Riverton Teachers Association. Oddly, Ross didn't look surprised to see him go.

Tyler Haden stopped at the outdoor entranceway, while officers Scaggs and Miller continued to take Mr. Moss to where his car was parked. The two officers stood there in silence as Mr. Moss climbed into his car. Brendan did not look up as he turned the key in the ignition and backed out of his space. Within seconds he had driven away.

The two Riverton Officers stood next to each other. Miller broke their silence.

"Something ain't right," he said to Dexter Scaggs who nodded in agreement.

Miller repeated himself, "Something ain't right."

Chapter 8

During the winter of 1964, Brendan and his dad were out buying a birthday gift for his mother. His father had run into a guy who had worked with him at the auto parts shop. While the two men talked, Brendan stood patiently nearby. His dad introduced Brendan to his friend and his father's coworker starting asking him some questions.

"So young man," the fellow asked, "what do you plan to be when you grow up?"

"I'm going to be an English teacher."

Brendan's Dad appeared impressed by his son's bold prediction. His friend was equally taken aback by the certainty of the kid's proclamation.

As a youngster, Brendan looked forward to the day where he would be in charge of his own classroom. But years later, this strong desire to teach would fade and he would need to be forced by his mother to attend a job interview for a teaching position. Today, he was glad he did. Teaching is an awesome job.

"Why do you want to be a teacher?"

Brendan shrugged his shoulders. He wasn't ready to share his reason why, although he of course knew. The reason was Mr. Blanda.

Mr. Blanda was Brendan's seventh grade English teacher, and for whatever the reason, teacher and student had developed a special relationship. Once, when Brendan made a disrespectful comment about another teacher, Mr. Blanda punished him severely by making him write a rather lengthy paragraph fifty times! It took Brendan over three hours to complete the spontaneous writing assignment, and when it was over, Brendan not only felt guilty about what he said, but grew worried that his favorite teacher would never like him again.

"So what team are you playing on Saturday?' Mr. Blanda had asked Brendan after class the following day. Brendan played basketball in the town league.

"We're playing the Hawks," he had answered a bit apprehensively, and when he looked up and saw that Mr. Blanda was smiling, he realized something; Mr. Blanda still liked him!

Young Brendan Moss learned something from Mr. Blanda that day that led him to be a better teacher himself in the future. In church, he once heard the preacher describe it this way: Hate the sin but never the sinner. Joe Blanda had believed in his potential. He liked him. When Mr. Blanda punished him, he didn't start liking Brendan less. Joe Blanda was addressing the behavior, not making an appraisal of the child.

Brendan never forgot those fifty paragraphs. He used Joe Blanda as his model for discipline, because he also liked the kids he taught. So many of his students needed him to like them, and also needed the discipline he was not afraid to dish out.

Many years after Mr. Blanda had long retired, and when Brendan was already an experienced math teacher himself, he and Emily were watching the Oprah Show. Oprah was discussing school teachers who had made a positive impact on the lives of their students. At the end of the show, Oprah suggested that viewers call their former teacher and thank them for the influence they had had and the role they played in helping them to become successful.

Brendan phoned Joe Blanda. Joe was pleasantly surprised to hear from his former student, and he laughed when he found out the motivation for the call. "Do you miss it?" Brendan asked the retired English teacher.

"No, not really," Mr. Blanda responded, "it's changed so much. Years ago, we teachers were looked up to and respected, our opinions were valued.

That's not the case anymore. Parents have changed. The support we once enjoyed is missing, and I don't think it will ever be the way it was again. Look at your mom and dad. They attended every event that you and your brothers were involved in. Our gym and auditorium used to be packed with families. That has all changed. Right before I retired, I noticed how so many of my students who participated in sports, band, and chorus didn't have a single family member present at their events to cheer them on. It's sad, and usually the only time you hear from this group of non-involved parents is when you discipline their child and they come in to complain. Education is not what it used to be. I don't know how you do it, Brendan. I'm glad I got out when I did."

And now Brendan was out. The first week of his administrative leave was a bit unnerving. He continued to wake early and work on his novel, but he missed teaching: the kids, the other teachers, being on a schedule. Staying home alone was not thrilling. Oh, perhaps if Emily were still around, it may have been lots of fun, but she wasn't.

By the second week, his attitude had changed. As Brendan took stock of his present situation, he realized there were some positive aspects to the situation. For one, he continued to receive his bi-weekly salary check. It really did not make sense. The Riverton School District was already dealing with a two million dollar budget deficit. By placing him on leave, the district would have to hire a substitute teacher and pay this individual between 80 and 100 dollars a day, while simultaneously offering him his full salary.

What were they up to? Why would any business, already in financial hot water, pay someone when they were not working? What was their goal? Brendan realized that Bailey Thompson wouldn't have risen to his position as superintendent if he wasn't a smart, capable man. The man had to be up to something, but what?

All he could do was collect his paychecks and wait. So instead of going to work early each morning, Brendan started waking up a little later to watch Sports Center. He would make a nice breakfast for himself, and then go to the YMCA to lift weights and play basketball. He began to accept the conditions of his paid vacation and made every effort to enjoy himself.

Back in Riverton, the staff was clueless as to why Brendan Moss, a thirty year teaching veteran, was escorted out of the building by Mr. Haden and two armed police officers. Rumors were swirling about an inappropriate relationship with a young girl, but not many people believed Mr. Moss would be romantically involved with a student. The idea of it was preposterous. Others presumed he was dismissed because of the incident with Oscar Campenelli. This idea caused the staff to grumble. Their thoughts on the issue were fairly unanimous. Oscar Campenelli deserved whatever he got!

During the first week of Brendan's administrative leave, Tyler Haden brought up the topic that was on everybody's mind. "I know I'm not permitted to say much, and I apologize for not coming to you all sooner, but due to the impending investigation, I am under order to only tell you what I can. Brendan Moss is on administrative leave until further notice. In the meantime, we are in the process of interviewing applicants for the eighth grade math position, due to the closeness of the state exam in April. This is all that I'm at liberty to share at this point, and once I am made privy to more information, you will all be the first to know."

The very intrigued group of middle school teachers remained silent following the principal's brief explanation. They knew as much now as they had before, but that was to be expected in Riverton. It seemed almost typical to have a dedicated staff member embarrassed by a string of accusations and to then have it explained away, by saying nothing!

The eighth grade English teacher, Maya Gregg, raised her hand, "What the hell is this all about, Tyler?"

It was the question everyone wanted to ask.

Haden's face turned red. "That's all I know."

Ms. Gregg shook her head, "We all love you Tyler, but you're not fooling anybody. I was there when Mr. Moss broke up the Campenelli fight. The only thing he was trying to do was protect Billy Weston. Mr. Moss was once my eighth grade teacher and I never sensed that he was inappropriate in any way. So as for this Richardson girl…."

"Excuse me, but I will not allow this sensitive topic to be discussed in a public forum," a voice called from behind them.

The blood drained from Tyler Haden's face as his eyes met those of the superintendent, Bailey Thompson. "I may be new here," Thompson declared strongly to the middle school staff, "but I refuse to tiptoe around basic philosophical issues. The foundation of my professional belief system is this: Riverton School District is here for the kids. This is not like other companies who prioritize their employees. We are for kids and about kids, and we will make every effort to make certain that what is best is based upon the children's needs and not the concerns of our faculty. It is my job to ensure that the young people here are protected and that this school, their school, is as safe a place for them as possible. For this reason, I granted an administrative leave for one of our teachers. I am familiar with the man's reputation, work ethic, and contributions to the community of Riverton, but as I said, we are not here to provide employment. We are here for the kids, and if there is even the slightest impropriety, or scent of suspicious behavior in an adult who is supposed to be role model what for what is good, just, and right, I will take the matter seriously! If there is no truth to our suspicions, then rest assured, your colleague will be reinstated and his reputation restored. However, no one is going to get away with harming kids on my watch. If Mother Teresa was accused of mistreating a child, she would also be placed on administrative leave."

A few listeners grinned at the analogy. Most people remained expressionless. No one was willing to challenge what they just heard.

"I like to think of myself," Thompson continued, "as a superintendent who backs his staff one-hundred percent."

It was like someone just hit Maya Gregg on the side of her head with a two-by-four. The superintendent was lying. It wasn't what the superintendent said or even how he said it that made her feel so certain, but she knew that she knew!

"I am here for you guys," Thompson reiterated. "I will stand by your side through your most difficult moments, but I will not choose your side over what I believe is best for a child. You may as well know this up front. I'm here for you, yes, but I am mostly here to help our young people in Riverton, and right now, we have an issue with serious implications to deal with. I promise you that I will be fair with everyone involved."

Once again intuition pricked Maya Gregg. It was another lie! The superintendent had no intention of being fair.

"Now as your superintendent, I sense that I must utilize my authority on your behalf. I need to institute a gag rule on any communication involving your dismissed colleague. I do not want anyone to talk about it with family, friends, or community members. We don't, as yet, have enough information to offer an educated opinion, so I am asking you to keep your thoughts to yourself, at least until more facts are brought to light."

He stopped. "Is that clear?"

Brendan Moss did not sleep well. He usually fell to sleep quickly after a busy day, even in spite of the lies and rumors circulating in Riverton. The drama, even the alarming news of Abby Richardson's transfer to a different school district, (how that must look), never disturbed his sleep, but his son, Jonathan, sitting an entire varsity basketball game on the bench did!

He was the only parent the kid had. With Emily gone from their lives for five years now, Brendan had to do all of the parenting. Amanda, of course, was out on her own now, married and seemingly doing well, and Jonathan, his lack of playing time aside, was never the cause of any worry.

But there was Matthew. His middle child was twenty-one years old, had already quit college twice, and was currently working at a pizza place in Ashton. At one point, he had considered joining the Navy, but he had met a girl named Heather and when they had started dating his career plans dissipated. Brendan knew that the couple was most likely sexually active, and while he didn't like that, he did like Heather. He knew that Matthew's struggle to find his purpose was common among youth, and he also knew that many of his concerns for his son were minor and would be resolved in time. His biggest worry was Matthew's attitude toward the Christian faith.

All three of the children were raised in a Christian home. He, Emily and the kids attended church each Sunday and were regularly involved in church related activities. The three kids were taught that the Bible was the infallible Word of God and that Jesus died for their sins. All three accepted the Lord as their personal Savior at a young age. That was important to both Brendan and Emily.

Then Mom died, and Brendan knew that the loss of her affected all of his children as much as it affected him. Brendan believed that the loss of his mother was one of the reasons that Matthew was no longer a believer.

His son often lovingly mocked his father for his Christian faith. When they discussed the Bible, the present life, or the life hereafter, his son's arguments of logic and sense seemed to trump Brendan's plea for faith.

"Dad," Matt had informed him one day, "I'm going to Washington, DC, for the weekend."

"What's going on there?"

"A bunch of us are going to an Anti-organized religion rally."?

Brendan did not like that answer, but what is a father to do? His agnostic son no longer believed in the God he and Emily had brought him up to trust and believe in. It hurt, but by faith, Brendan Moss stuck to this conviction: Matthew Moss will remember his childhood commitment to Jesus. There was not much Brendan could do, but pray. Matt needed protection and God would have to be the one to protect his son.

Jonathan, on the other hand, was more agreeable. Oh, it was virtually impossible to get his youngest to go to church either, but at least Jon was open to the concept of faith. Tonight however, it was not the soul of his child that tormented him.

Jonathan was a talented player who sat the bench. On many occasions, the boy never even entered the game. It bothered Brendan to no end. One day he spoke to a friend of his, Stephen, about how he was considering speaking to the coach about it.

"Don't do it!" Stephen commanded him. "Your son is on a team by his own will. No one made him sign up. I'm guessing that he wants to be there. The team is not there for your son. Jon is there for the team, and your job as his father is to support the team. Cheer for them, encourage the boys that you tell me are always over at your house, and let the chips fall where they may."

So that's just what Brendan did, but man, it was hard. It was a question of boundaries. As a parent of a varsity basketball player, what were his boundaries? What he thought he should be able to do and what he was allowed to do were certainly in opposition to each other. Brendan knew in his heart that Jon was talented enough to play, and play well at the varsity level. As a former basketball coach himself, Brendan trusted in his ability to judge talent. He was not a father who blindly viewed his children's capabilities with rose-colored glasses. No, Jon was a player, but a player who rarely played.

Brendan recited what he wanted to say to the varsity coach over and over again in his mind. He felt that he had facts and statistics that he could use to educate the coach. He knew what he wanted to say. He just didn't know if he had the right to say it.

It was now his habit to sit alone at games. When his older son Matthew had played, the boy had started and was on the court nearly every minute. Brendan and Emily would freely join a group of other parents and cheer loudly for the boys. Now with Jon riding the pines, he decided it was best to sit alone. This way, his emotional despair would not spoil the atmosphere for the other parents. Brendan remembered what it was like when Matt played. Each game was an event and the excitement of varsity competition engulfed him. He never missed a game.

Regrets are funny. He wished now that he had stayed home, instead of going to see his son play on the evening of January 30th, 2006. Brendan thought that it would be nice if God put a red light on our foreheads to warn us: proceed with caution. Perhaps then we could avoid regret, by knowing ahead of time what might happen.

Emily rarely had complained of pain. She had a history of migraines, but otherwise she had been strong and healthy. Perhaps it was just a bad day.

The night of the 29th, she'd gone to bed early, because in her own words, she just wasn't feeling right. Twice during the night she had gotten up to go to the bathroom to throw up. The third time she rose, Brendan had followed her.

"This is the worst headache I've ever had."

"Should we go to the ER?" His voice betrayed his increasing concern.

"I'll be fine. It's probably just the flu."

Brendan had stayed home from school to be with her. His wife had remained listless for most of the morning, but by the late afternoon and early evening, she seemed to be making a recovery. Brendan remained with her in their bedroom, when Matthew Moss entered the room.

"I'm going," he said, informing his parents that he had to be at the school before the JV game. He turned to his mother, "Are you feeling okay?"

"Listen," Brendan began. "We might not be there tonight. Mom is still not quite right, so I'd better stay back with her."

"No," Emily shook her head, "I'll be fine. Go to the game. My God," she managed her first smile in twenty four hours, "you live for these games. You go. Tell me about it later."

There was only twenty-one seconds left in Matt's game. Ashton was trailing 62-60, but had possession of the ball. From the movement on the court, Brendan surmised that the coach was banking on JR, the team's strongest shooter, to win or tie the game.

With less than ten seconds remaining, it became evident that JR was in trouble. He threw the ball back beyond the three-point line where Matthew Moss stood unguarded. Matt caught the ball with two seconds left. He had to shoot.

As soon as the ball left his hand, the crowd rose to their feet. They all watched as the ball sailed right through the hoop for a game-winning three-pointer. Brendan jumped in the air! The Ashton players stormed the court and lifted Matthew Moss onto their shoulders! What a game! What a shot!

"I can't wait to tell your Mom," Brendan said, as he turned to Matt on the ride home.

He had made the next turn at the corner onto their street. There was an ambulance in a driveway with its lights flashing. Terror had choked him. It was his driveway.

Jonathan played over twelve minutes in his next game and even scored eight points, his first points of the season. As he moved down the steps of the bleachers after the game, Brendan noticed that a rather tall young man appeared to be handing out brochures to fans as they were leaving. It was Buster McHale.

"Hi, Mr. Moss."

"Hi, Buster."

Brendan's mind was in a fog. What was Buster doing here in Ashton? Didn't Riverton have a game tonight also?

"Don't you have a game tonight?" He couldn't help but ask.

"I quit the basketball team," Buster said as his smile faded. "After all that happened with Myles, the last thing I wanted was for people to cheer for me. I don't deserve to be cheered."

His earnest comment disturbed Brendan. Buster McHale had been a bully by his own choice. He was partially correct. He was not someone to cheer for. But the kid was also partially wrong. Brendan thought every kid should be built up, bullies included.

It had already been a few months since Myles' suicide. Things around Riverton had settled down, and the word was that the bullying, even at the high school level, was under stricter control. That was good news.

Brendan noticed that Buster was wearing a white shirt with a cross in the center. The print over the cross said "Ashton Methodist Church", and below read "Pastor Ronald Langston". "Have you been going to church there?" Brendan asked incredulously.

Buster explained, "Right after Christmas, Pastor Ronald paid me a visit. He asked how I was doing, what I was up to, and he even talked sports with me. When I told him that I had decided not to play basketball this season, we started talking about what had happened with Myles."

On both sides people were filing out of the gymnasium. Brendan barely noticed the commotion around him. What he was hearing from Buster McHale was keeping his full and complete attention.

"He forgave me, Mr. Moss. He invited me out to lunch. We talked about Myles, but you know what, Mr. Moss? He wasn't laying a guilt trip on me or anything like that. He just wanted to talk about his son. I guess he chose me for the obvious reasons. Here I do what I did," he stammered, "and he reaches out to me. He just lost his only son, and yet he wants to help me! Can you believe it? Well," Buster sniffed loudly, "I couldn't help but respond to that kind of love. I guess in the past few weeks I kind of let Pastor Ron adopt me. We pray together; I gave my heart to the Lord, and now I'm in the worship band at the church. Did you know I played the drums, Mr. Moss?'

What? Brendan's mind was racing. He had to take a moment to get his facts straight.

Fact 1: Buster McHale bullied poor, deceased Myles Langston unmercifully.

Fact 2: The emotionally depressed Myles shot himself in the head.

Fact 3: Buster quit the basketball team because of his feelings of guilt.

Fact 4: The very real Jesus Christ forgave him.

Fact 5: The Langstons forgave him.

Wait a minute. There's something wrong with fact 5.

At the funeral a very distraught Rae Langston, mother of the deceased child, attacked Buster McHale in her deeply felt anguish. Not once during his story of forgiveness from Pastor Ronald Langston did Buster mention the wife. Brendan tried to rewind what the kid said. He was right! Each time he referred to Myles' family he had said he, him and Pastor. Never once did Buster suggest that Rae Langston was a part of the reconciliation. Those were the facts.

"I want to thank you for being there for me, Mr. Moss. You're the only person who knows the truth about me. Do you remember I called you the night before? I was already going to change before he did it! The Lord knows that too. I will have to live the rest of my life with that regret. If only I had seen a day earlier what a monster I was! Perhaps the world would be different for me."

Brendan could identify with that last statement. He'd been there. He'd lived with his own regrets for over five years now. If he had only seen it coming a day earlier, perhaps the world would be different for him too.

By the time he had thrown the car into park and hurried towards the house, the medics were wheeling Emily out on a stretcher. He had rushed to her side.

"Please sir," an EMT said firmly, "we need to get her to the hospital as quickly as we can."

Another man held his arm out to shield Brendan and block potential interference.

"Are you the husband?"

His mouth was so dry that he was unable to verbally answer. Brendan nodded his head.

"You can ride along with us."

"Who got a hold of you?" Brendan asked.

"A neighbor called."

They were at the game. Brendan had turned off his cell phone.

Brendan turned to Amanda, "Take the boys into the house. I will call you as soon as I know something."

"We want to come too, Dad."

"All right," he hurriedly agreed. "Tell Matt to take my car, and I'll meet you guys at the hospital."

Brendan climbed into the back of the ambulance. The medics shut the door behind him. He sat on the right side of the stretcher that held his wife. He reached for her hand and held it tightly. Then Brendan whispered her name.

There was no response. He knew she wouldn't last the night right there and then.

Yet even though he knew, Brendan began to pray to the only One he knew who could help him. He sobbed while he prayed. He cried out for all to hear, hoping beyond hope that the One who could do something also heard. The two paramedics seated across from him started to cry too. Still Brendan Moss kept on, begging the Lord to show His miraculous power.

He had heard. Now what would He answer?

There was no response.

Why did I go to the game? My wife was ill. Why would I leave her all alone? It was just a high school basketball game!

Emily Moss died on the way to the hospital. The cause of death was a brain aneurism. A huge part of Brendan Moss also started dying that day. The cause of death was a broken heart, and the chief symptom was regret.

"I'm so proud of you, Buster." Brendan just had to tell the boy. "I know you feel guilty for the things you used to do." He stressed the words, "used to". "But even though nothing either of us can do will ever bring Myles back," Brendan gulped, "we still have the power to affect our society and community in a very positive way. God needs you, Buster. He wants you to take your bullying experiences and share them along with all the guilt and shame, and help put a stop to it!" My God, Brendan was thinking; I sound like a prophet! "If you need a platform I will help you."

"I might do some preaching."

Brendan was forced to clench his cheeks. Buster's declaration moved him. Former Hall of Fame baseball player, Yogi Berra, said once: "It ain't over until it's over". Amen, how true! Buster McHale had a real chance to redeem himself and to be redeemed! We all do! Some have it tougher than others, but everybody can turn their lives around. Even Myles Langston could have had a better life if he'd stayed around long enough to give himself a chance.

"So what are you handing out?" Brendan asked Buster, remembering that when he first saw him he was distributing some kind of literature.

"Our church is having a tent revival in two week," Buster declared enthusiastically. "Pastor Ronald sent a bunch of us to different games tonight to hand them out. I guess I could have stayed in Riverton, but I asked Pastor If I could hand them out in Ashton instead."

"Why?"

Buster smiled, "I wanted to give a flyer to you, Mr. Moss." The kid paused to let his preference have its desired effect. "I'm going to be one of the speakers under the tent, and I was hoping you would be there."

That's one of the great things about being a teacher. If you remain in teaching long enough, some of the kids will honor you. They may do it with their words or by their actions, but through the years the salutes will come.

"I wouldn't miss it for the world."

Just then a young lady joined them. Brendan recognized her as one of his former students. Her name was Alexa Hughes, and while she was an attractive young woman, the National Honor Society member was also considered a geek.

'Alexa is with Buster?' wondered Brendan.

"Hi, Mr. Moss."

Alexa Hughes was a great girl. She was the president of the Junior Class and in the fall had started a club for young Christians called, 'The Disciples'. She was everything that was good about youth. A couple of months ago Alexa wouldn't have stood with a bully like Buster McHale, and now they were friends?

Seeing the two of them together gave Brendan a good feeling. It gave him a shot of hope. Maybe, just maybe, everything in life is going to turn out to be all right, just like the Bible says.

He shook his head. *Wow! What's next?*

"So what's next?"

Dan Ross, president of the RTA, leaned heavily upon his elbows as he asked the question. Across from him sat two men. One of the men was Bailey Thompson, and the other man he knew by his reputation.

The other man answered.

"We revoke his tenure, but we still have to be careful. The complaints against him won't stand in a law court, but if we can set the precedent that teachers should not be guaranteed jobs for life, well then, we've accomplished our goal."

"Thank you for coming to Riverton, Mr. Haines," Thompson coughed as he stood to shake the Commissioner of Education's hand.

Robert Haines was in the Western New York area to visit a number of schools on a sort of good will tour. Things were not good in education in the state of New York, so the Commissioner was out encouraging the most misaligned districts. Riverton was one of the districts on the list, and here the Commissioner's visit had a second purpose.

Before leaving, Haines turned back to Dan Ross and gave him a knowing wink and a smile.

"We'll keep in touch. I think you will work well in Albany."

With that he left.

Charles Hayes never saw it coming.

He was still dressing in the locker room after gym, and while lacing his shoes, a force shoved him forward. The top of his head struck the locker in front of him, as his body tumbled to the ground. First straightening his glasses, Charles looked up to see who had pushed him.

It was Oscar Campanelli.

Since the middle school boys shared the same locker room as the high school boys, the schedules allowed for separate periods of use to avoid cohabitation. There was no reason for Oscar Campenelli to be in the locker room during a time reserved for high school students, but he had been sent down to the office by his English teacher, and had gone to hide out there instead.

Charles quickly gathered himself after Oscar pushed him to the ground. He was used to this type of physical taunting by now, but it was still difficult to handle. He didn't know who this boy was, although he'd certainly seen him before. Charles placed his hands on his hips in an attempt to assume a position of control, but inside he was very nervous. There wasn't an adult in sight. This could be bad.

"What do you want?" Charles demanded, stirring up enough bravado to respond.

"I want you," Oscar answered strongly, and he wasn't nervous.

Charles braced himself for the attack. He could tell that this younger kid meant business, and that he was mean enough to see it through. Charles was ready. He gritted his teeth and clenched his fist. And then he smiled.

Oscar Campenelli felt the front of his shirt yanked up towards his neck. Buster McHale's hand was at his back and he heard him ask Charles, "Is he bothering you?"

Soon after the tragedy, Buster had made it a point to seek out Charles. He apologized and asked Charles for forgiveness, which he granted. The two of them now got together once in a while to go for a run. It was Charles' idea.

"You are a gifted athlete," Charles implored, after hearing that Buster had quit the basketball team. "God gave you that special ability. Use it, man!"

But Buster persisted, so Charles suggested, "At least go for a run with me once in a while, just to stay in shape." So Buster agreed, and he was surprised by his inability to keep up with the little guy.

"Before I send you back to the middle school," Buster directed Oscar, "I want you to understand something. You need help. I know because I've been there. I used to get my kicks pushing around kids I was bigger and stronger than too. No one understands you better than I do. You and I are similar, Oscar Campenelli. We pick on others, because we've got our own major issues. We're hurting inside, and our pain is deep. I didn't even know why I picked on kids. I just did it. You probably just do it." Buster gently put both his hands on Oscar's shoulders. Oscar didn't like that one bit. "But you're not going to bother my friend, Charles. Now get back where you belong, because I'm still a work in progress. Beware: I still have anger issues."

With that, Buster removed his hands from Oscar's shoulders and gently tapped the boy's chest, "I'm sure we won't need to talk about this again."

Campenelli turned to leave the locker room, but an evil scowl marked his face and he mocked, "Like I would listen to a murderer!"

That hurt. It always hurt anytime someone or something reminded him. It was Charles' turn to come to the rescue. "I don't care what anybody says about you. I know the real Buster McHale, and I know what a kind, caring person you are. What happened has happened. I will not defend who you once chose to be. I'm glad he's gone," Charles smiled, "but the guy you are today, I would defend to the death if I had to." His voice was showing some emotion. "You have no idea how much I admire you, Buster. You will make a difference around here. I know I'm right."

"Do you know that I hate it in there?" Buster leaned his head back towards the locker room. " It used to be my most favorite place on earth, now I'm almost afraid to go in."

Charles grew quite serious, "The devil always tries to remind us of what we used to be. Jesus paid for all of that. The Bible says, 'There's no longer any condemnation for those who are in Christ'. That's you, man. I don't care what the world sees or says about you. You are clean. I try to see you the way God does, and," Charles added, with his eyebrows raised to feign disbelief, "even I still find it hard to believe, but I think it's one of the coolest things ever!"

Chapter 9

Brendan Moss had stood in front of the full length mirror that he had purchased for his wife.

"If you expect me to look beautiful, I'm going to need a full-length mirror so I can see myself."

"Look into my eyes," Brendan had said that day, years ago. "I'll be your mirror." He had smiled and held out his arms, "How do you look?"

"My God!" Emily Moss put her hands to her cheeks as she had recognized that special look on her husband's face. "I'm beautiful!"

Now the mirror was his.

Matthew came into the bedroom, looking for a tie to borrow. "Wear my red one." Brendan instructed, as he looked at himself in his all black suit. 'Is this actually happening?' he thought. The past two days had been pure hell in one sense, but meeting and greeting old family and friends meant keeping busy. There was a lot to feel grateful for.

The funeral was packed. The line of mourners never seemed to end. It was nice to see so many people in attendance, and it was nice to be distracted. More than once, he questioned the reality of his words and movements as he looked around the funeral parlor and asked himself: *Is this really what I'm doing today?*

The answer of course was yes. Yes, Brendan Moss, you are now a widower.

Brendan tried to allow his life to return to normal. Amanda went back to college, while Matthew and Jonathan resumed school and sports, but he could not get Emily out of his mind. He told Tyler Haden that he was resigning, and that the middle school principal should advertise the open position. Haden however, had not believed for a moment that Mr. Moss meant what he said, and had instead hired a long-term substitute teacher until his emotionally distraught math teacher decided to return.

A month later, Brendan did return. He grew weary of seeing the rooms without her in them, and realized that his own apathetic existence wasn't doing anyone any good. So he resumed his post.

On his very first day back, he walked in on a sixth grader pulling a victim's pants down to his knees. Other kids looking on roared their approval. He and Maya Gregg quieted the crowd, as she escorted the tall sixth grade boy to the office.

When she returned, she walked over to Brendan and laughed, "Welcome back, Mr. Moss. You can see things haven't changed much around here."

"Who was that boy?"

Maya Gregg rolled her eyes. "He makes trouble everywhere he goes."

Brendan shook his head, "Someone for us to look forward to, huh?"

"Oh, I don't know," Maya adopted a different tone. "There's something about him that makes me think he could be something special."

"Really?" Brendan had asked incredulously. "What's his name?"

"Buster McHale."

Raleigh McDevitt, the Governor of New York, very grimly addressed the reporters gathered in Albany. His message was blunt and ominous. Grant funding, valued at $800 million, and designated for New York public schools districts, was currently in jeopardy. New York was among the top three states on the federal government's watch list, following repeated failures to comply with set goals. The lack of development in a teacher and principal evaluation system, would lead to a law suit.

Governor McDevitt's speech sounded more like a warning. "This is just another example of how the inability of school districts and their teachers' unions to come together has jeopardized the quality of our kids' education. New York State students are now in danger of losing hundreds of millions of dollars, because our school districts have failed to devise a teacher evaluation system that works."

Many members of the state teachers association were present. Following the Governor's announcement of potential loss of government funding, Linda Malachi, President of the NEA, sent this e-mail to every school district in New York.

"Once again Albany is trying to blame us for student's failing grades. Our failure to form a new teacher evaluation system by the agreed upon date is mostly the result of an unrealistic time frame set by lawmakers. They truly do not understand what it means to negotiate.

Our previous evaluation system has been invalidated, since it did not take test scores into account. The new requirement for the inclusion of test scores is frightening, because it is a means of measure that is outside of our control. The governor wants forty percent of the evaluation to be based on test scores.

Each school has a different set of needs and traditions, and an evaluation system should ideally be molded to fit the conditions of each unique district. Let's face it. The information we are receiving from the State Education Department is either conflicting or vague. This makes it difficult to understand the parameters of the new requirements. For now, please wait for me to instruct you on what needs to be done next."

In Riverton, Tyler Haden leaned back in his chair after reading the e-mail from Linda Malachi. He sighed and thought of Brendan Moss. What *a political mess education was in!*

A tent revival in the middle of winter was unprecedented in Western New York. It was cold and snowy, but Pastor Ronald Langston told his congregation that he'd heard from God, and the Lord wanted a revival now! Riverton was certainly a town in need.

The community was still reeling from the suicide of the Pastor's son, Myles, and the doom and gloom atmosphere over the town had settled like a thick fog. Not many people in Riverton knew the Langston family well, but the same could be said for Jesus. People were down and depressed, and unsure as to how to change the mood. Ronald Langston sensed the spiritual darkness and prayed to God for a solution. The Lord's answer was a tent revival.

There were lots of portable heaters in place and Mother Nature lent a hand by providing unseasonably warmer winter temperatures. Over two hundred wooden folding chairs were placed in rows and rented lighting was positioned. The first night attracted nearly one hundred people. A large percentage of those gathered were worshippers, but the lighted tent in the middle of the winter also attracted a number of curious, non-religious town members.

There were around twenty high school students in attendance the first night. The kids enjoyed what they saw and heard. Only a few of the youngsters had ever been to a church service before, so the upbeat praise band, stirring messages of hope and joy, caught their collective interest.

Buster McHale was scheduled to speak in the early evening of the second and final night of the revival. When one of the high school kids saw a poster advertising the event, he enthusiastically informed his group of friends. The word spread quickly.

"Do you believe it, Mr. Moss?" One of Brendan's math students shared the startling news. "Buster McHale is that big kid who made that little boy shoot himself. Man, I want to hear what he has to say about that."

Brendan didn't respond to the kid's enthusiasm about hearing the details of Myles' death, but he could not deny that he was also interested. He agreed that a lot of young people wanted to hear what Buster McHale was going to say.

Brendan followed the crowd of high school and middle school students to the tent for the second night of the revival. He found a seat and waited. He had asked his two sons to join him, but both had declined. It was hard to get his children to attend anything with him that had to do with church or God, but he would certainly keep asking.

Buster McHale stood off to the right beside Pastor Ronald Langston. Brendan had heard from Buster that the Pastor had reached out to him, but this was the first time he'd witnessed it with his own eyes. People always say that seeing is believing. Well, sometimes even what you can see can be hard to believe. Buster and Pastor Langston fell into that category.

Brendan watched as Pastor Langston pulled Buster towards him and gave the kid a hug. Then the Pastor patted the kid on his back a couple of times in encouragement. Brendan's eyes instantly filled with tears. What he'd already witnessed was worth his effort to attend. Brendan loved people for their one consistency, the ability to surprise.

Buster McHale tapped the microphone and surveyed the crowd. He wasn't the least bit nervous. He was excited! He saw a number of faces that he recognized from school. He was glad they were here.

"Ladies and gentlemen," he began with the normal introductory protocol, "my name is Buster McHale, and I would like to share my story with you. I'm a bully," Buster started. "I hurt people because I think it is fun. I seek them out, plan my attacks, and wait until a time that I sense I can get away with it. I don't care about my victims. It doesn't matter to me how much they hurt as a result of my actions. I only care about one thing, and that's me."

"That's not true!"

Towards the rear of the tent, Charles Hayes had risen to his feet to make his interruptive declaration. He had no intention of causing a scene, but when he didn't like what he was hearing, he just couldn't help himself.

"Tell it the way it is, Buster. You used to be a bully. You used to hurt people, and you used to care only about yourself. You're not that guy anymore."

Brendan Moss felt his lower lip quiver. He was so proud of both of them. It was a moment of pride that he would cherish forever. To think that he was once their teacher! To think that he had such a positive influence on their young lives. Wow!

"Thank you, Charles," Buster said as he pointed a finger at his new friend. "You're right. They are all 'used to be' situations." He cleared his throat, "My new friend, Charles Hayes, is trying to protect me. He doesn't want me to feel bad about myself. He thinks that I'm beating myself up over what is now in the past, but he really doesn't quite understand what it is I need to do. He cares about me," Buster smiled a sad smile, "but I have to say what I have to say, and I'm going to do just that. So please Charles, don't interrupt me again."

There was scattered laughter throughout the tent.

"A young man in our community took his own life as a direct result of my bullying tactics. We can sugarcoat it all we like, and say that there were other issues he was dealing with, but the bottom line is this: I'm the cause of this tragedy. Right after I victimized Myles Langston I experienced an epiphany. I left the school that day, and for the first time I saw the monster that I once was." He exchanged glances with Charles as he accentuated the word *once*. "I decided right then and there that my life, attitude, and actions were going to change. I would bully no more. I even phoned a former teacher to inform him of my decision."

This was all too much for Brendan Moss. As he sat listening to Buster bare his soul, tears ran down his cheek. It was so, so sad. Yet at the same time, hearing the boy's confession was so, so good. "I talked to the teacher that night, and he wisely recommended that I search out Myles the following morning and ask him for his forgiveness. I planned to do just that. Only," he stumbled, "there would be no tomorrow morning in the life of Myles Langston."

Buster's sniffling instantly turned to sobs, and he wasn't the only one. People, young and old, were sobbing right along with him. Brendan Moss just wanted to jump up and run away! He felt like he couldn't listen to this a moment longer.

"God tells us in his Word," Buster began when he was finally able to speak again, "that none of us knows how much time we have left. Time and chance affect everybody. So I made a decision a few days after Myles Langston's funeral. I must confess, leading up to the funeral, I thought about joining him." A gasp was heard from the crowd. "I seriously considered taking my own life, because I hated who I was, what I did, and believed that I would forever regard myself as worthless. A part of me," he admitted, "still does."

Buster stopped for a moment and opened the Bible on the podium.

"In Chapter 23 of the Book of Luke, Jesus is on the cross between two criminals. The Bible doesn't tell us exactly what the bad guys did, but whatever it was, they were guilty and deserved their punishment. One of them in verse 42 says to Jesus, 'Lord, remember me when you come into your kingdom'. Jesus answers back, 'Assuredly, I say to you, today you will be with me in Paradise'."

He couldn't help himself. Brendan knew exactly where the kid was going with all of this, so he got to his feet, closed his eyes, tilted his head back, and raised both arms. He was praising God. If the speaker noticed, he made no indication. By the time Buster resumed, Brendan had sat back down.

"This guy on the cross next to Jesus had no opportunity to redeem himself. He was cooked! He had no chance to pay back those he'd robbed, or to ever seek forgiveness from those he injured. The only thing he had left to do was to die. He did not get a second chance to improve himself as a person. He was never given the opportunity to stand in front of a crowd to share his story." Buster paused again, "I do."

Buster took a moment to look out over the gathering. He spotted many individuals that he'd shoved, ridiculed, or humiliated in the past. In most cases, he didn't even know their names. But to his surprise he did recognize one of the young men who stood in the back. Who would have ever thought that he would be here! He thought to himself: God is so amazing! "The convict on the cross did not have a chance to prove that he was a changed man. He didn't tell his family or friends about it. Yet as this criminal passed from this life to the next, Jesus was waiting to welcome him. Now that's love! I have, God willing, a lot more time to live here on this earth than that fellow did, and I promise you this, I'm going to make the best of it.

"It's not easy to be me right now. I'll be frank: I hate myself. I know what the Bible says about forgiveness, redemption, and the renunciation of sins. I know too, that Jesus has pronounced me worthy to die for. I know all this. In fact, during the last few weeks, I believe that the Lord has spoken to me and suggested that I consider being a preacher or an evangelist, but I have other ideas. Even though I know that God cares about me, I still hate myself.

"You see, God only suggests that we follow the plans he has for our individual lives. He never makes us do anything. I was a bully, and I need to make this part very clear. I was not a bully, because I couldn't help myself. No, I was a bully, because I wanted to be a bully. I bullied, because I was bigger and stronger, and I knew that in Riverton, as long as I kept scoring touchdowns and making three-pointers, no one was going to stop me.

"A month after Myles Langston died; there was a knock at my door. I remember it well. I was upstairs in my room, anguishing over my decision to quit the basketball team. My parents were out, so I had to answer the door. To my shock, it was Myles Langston's father. My heart stopped when I recognized him," Buster recalled, "I first thought that he came for revenge. I invited him in and we talked for over an hour. I cried like a babbling baby. I cried so much that I could barely catch my breath. My chest was on fire. At one point it got so bad that Pastor Ronald feared for my life."

Once again Buster began to cry. Brendan Moss buried his face into his hands momentarily before lifting it up to stare at the huge young man behind the podium. He made a spontaneous decision. This was too hard for a seventeen year old to do alone. So Brendan got out of his seat, strode into the aisle, and started walking towards the stage. When he got to the front, Brendan moved to his left to ascend a short flight of stairs. He stood close to the boy.

Buster understood immediately that Mr. Moss was telling him, "I am with you". It was just what the kid needed to continue.

"The buzz word throughout our talk was forgiveness. I have no idea how this man found it in his heart to forgive me, the guy who led his own son to suicide, but he did! And he meant it. Pastor wasn't just playing or acting out a role because the Bible commands him to do so. He forgave me because he cared about me, was worried about me, and mostly because he knew I needed to know that there is a God who forgives."

Buster paused again. "Please hear me as I share what happened last week. It was during social studies class, and a boy was answering a question about the Ming Dynasty. He got nervous and started to stutter. I was tempted to poke fun at him. My mind was churning with derisive quips. I even considered mimicking him. That's the battle that goes on inside of me! I want to bully. It's like there's this thing or force within me, that I think I can't control, and I can't on my own, but now," Buster's eyes widened, "I have a new source of power inside of me. His name is Jesus, and when I want to ridicule, embarrass, harass, or bully He gives me the strength and self-control to say no! I hope that as I continue to practice listening to Him, that someday I won't have to fight so hard. It'll be real. I will love people. I will want to do the right thing, and I will take this compulsion to bully, rip it to shreds, and be done with it!"

Unexpectedly, people began to applaud. Brendan Moss, standing silently beside the young speaker, applauded also. People heard something they liked, and something inside of them responded. A good portion even rose to their feet.

"I have issues," Buster's took up again, louder, "and I will always carry the pain of knowing that my actions cost a young kid his life, but I promise you, I will press on. God gifted me with the ability to play sports, so I will play baseball this spring. Only, playing games will never be what it once was. I used to play for myself, for personal acclaim and recognition. I've heard applause before. I relished it after scoring a touchdown or hitting a homerun. I know what it's like to receive approval, but the applause I received just minutes ago was the most meaningful applause that I have ever received, because it was directed towards the real Buster McHale, and I will cherish that moment in my life forever. Unlike the prisoner on the cross beside Jesus, I still have a great opportunity to straighten out my life and help make a positive change. Bullies are dangerous. We need to deal with it. Myles Langston did not have to die."

Buster McHale looked over at his bodyguard, Mr. Moss, and motioned for him to move closer. Brendan did as instructed. Buster moved to the side of the podium to face his former math teacher. "It means a lot to me that you came up to support me, Mr. Moss. Let me tell you what I found out about Myles Langston," Buster said, as though Mr. Moss was the only person he was addressing. "Myles planned on going to college to become an air traffic controller. Those are the guys who make sure that planes land safely. That way, passengers can be confident that they will reach their destination and see their loved ones. It's a very important job, Mr. Moss, and I imagine that a person has to be very smart and very caring to do that kind of work. Pastor Ronald told me that his son won a few scholastic awards. He was proud of him. You know," Buster made an odd face, attempting to control the twitching muscles around his cheeks, "I learned lots about Myles from his father. Myles loved planes and birds. He liked to draw, play music, and he even *enjoyed* math and science. Myles was comfortable in the classroom. His dad told me that Myles really enjoyed your class especially. He said it wasn't just because of the math, but because he felt safe in your room. He trusted that if any bullies so much as glanced sideways at him, that you would deal with it and protect him. I remember that I knew that too, and I used to hate you for it!" He grimaced. "It's unbelievable to us, Mr. Moss, that of all the teachers at Riverton, they get rid of you. What are they thinking?

Everybody knows you're innocent. You are suffering when you are innocent, while I suffer as a guilty man."

"You used to be guilty!" a voice shouted out. It was Charles Hayes.

Buster spun back towards the podium.

"Good point, Charles," he acknowledged. "In fact," now Buster focused on the crowd, "that's exactly what I need to talk about. Pastor Ronald didn't come to my house to only forgive me and tell me about Myles. Oh no," Buster shook his head, "he had a whole other message to share."

Everybody knew what was coming next. After all, this was a revival meeting. "Life is hard, and going through it alone is almost impossible. Listen to me: I'm the lowest of the low. I have hurt people badly. I was not a good person. Yet," he paused for effect, "Jesus took me and accepted me just the way I am.

"I want all you high school people to hear me. Maybe you came tonight, because it's preposterous that Buster McHale, of all people, would be preaching, and you just had to see it with your own eyes. Perhaps it was simply curiosity that brought you here. Or so you think! I've learned a lot from Pastor Ronald these past couple of months, and one of the things I've learned is this. We're not where we are by accident! God got you to be here tonight. He has something to say to you. This revival is not about the trials and tribulations, and hopeful redemption of Buster McHale. This is about you! I'm one of you. I know the difficulties you face. I know them firsthand. It's not easy to be a teenager. Look," Buster apologized, "I'm new at this evangelism stuff, so here's all I know: Jesus is real! He paid the price for our sins. We get to cash in on this incredible once in a lifetime deal by just saying yes to His offer. They call it the Great Exchange. You give Jesus all your crap," Buster stopped for a split second, unsure if his word choice was appropriate, "You give Him your fears, your anger, the things you just can't deal with, your family issues, your addiction, or whatever else is dragging you down. Bullying other kids is not the answer. Joining a gang is not an answer. Suicide is not the answer!"

Buster lowered his head and took a deep breath. When he looked up, his eyes blazed with determination. "I don't wish to sound all theological, so let me just tell you about my personal experience with Jesus. I listened to everything Pastor Ronald had to say, and somewhere in my spirit was the conviction to say yes. There were no visions, no angels with wings flying around the room, and to be perfectly honest with you; I felt nothing! I still don't *feel* any different, but there has been a change. Those of you who know me, or at the very least know of me, have recognized the change. My God, I'm standing on a stage at a revival meeting and preaching!" His comment brought about a smattering of laughter. "Did anyone seriously visualize that back in September? And even more incredible than that, is that Mr. Moss is standing beside me to lend his support."

Once again Buster focused his full and sole attention on Mr. Moss. "Here's how I know I've changed. You were the one teacher I hated the most. I hated your rules and high expectations, and when I misbehaved, I especially hated your persistence to see my punishment to the end. I used to laugh when after you gave me my punishment, the school administrators would let me tell my side and set me free, while you would be reprimanded for too severely dealing with a student. You would give me what I deserved and they would stop you! You knew what was right, and come hell or high water, you were going to do your best to see that what was right won out. There were plenty of times I wanted to take a swing at you. You got in my way, Mr. Moss. I would look at you and disdainfully think: 'Who do you think you are? You're just a math teacher.' It was only recently that I've come to see how you view your chosen profession.

" You don't see it as just a job, you believe that if you just keep trying, keep reaching out to us, or if you refuse to let our behavior and bad attitude deter you, that you just might reach a few of us. You decided to look past our selfishness, our collective, almost gang-like mentality, and instead you search us for something else. You didn't care if we liked you. You were going to try and do what's best for us, no matter what, and we fought you.

"When I had you in the eighth grade, you made the same speech, at least a dozen times. You'd start out by telling us how the teachers were the good guys. You explained how you guys were there to point us in the right direction. You knew you were right, and no matter how many times we dissed you, made fun of you, mimicked you, or cussed you to your face; you just kept plugging away. You never gave up on us. And I learned something recently: Jesus is the same way."

Buster turned away from his little private chat with Mr. Moss, and faced the audience once again. Since he had no idea that Mr. Moss would walk up to the stage to support him, his dialogue with the middle school math teacher was totally unrehearsed, but it did go rather well, and Buster was intrigued by how easily it related to what he had to say next.

"At every church service, Pastor Langston has what is known as an altar call. I am going to do the same. Here's what it is: If you're tired of the life you've been leading, fed up with the pain and confusion, and dissatisfied with the things you do and the way you live, then please, come up to the stage and myself, or one of Pastor Langston's staff, will pray for you. Come up and ask Jesus into your heart. He will change you! Oh, He's not going to do it all for you, but He will forgive your sins, and He will welcome you into His Kingdom. Trust me friends," Buster focused his invitation on the crowd of young people, "it's worth it."

The response was immediate. First a few young girls got out of their seats and made their way forward. Then a couple more, boys and girls, did the same. Within a minute, more than twenty Riverton High School students were on their feet and ready for a changed life. Two of the bigger boys were renowned bullies. One of the girls who came forward was a teenage mother who wanted her child to have a mother he would respect.

Buster McHale had expected a handful of students to come forward, but he was amazed to find Oscar Campenelli among them. Buster immediately went up to him, placed a gentle hand on his shoulder, and started to beseech the Lord to forgive and accept this particular young man into His Glorious Kingdom.

Afterwards a reporter from the Riverton Press approached McHale. "That was a terrific speech you made, young man. Are you going to be a preacher someday?"

Buster smiled and shook his head. "No," Buster explained sincerely, "I don't believe God has called me to preach."

"So what do you plan to do with your life?"

Buster smiled again, and as he did so he locked eyes with Mr. Moss.

"I want to be a school teacher."

The mood in the high school library was somber. Superintendent Thompson had made his bold suggestion, and now the members of the school board were expected to vote. Seven of the eight board members were present. Simon Tanner was missing only because his son was playing a basketball game in Ashton.

"All of those in favor?" Mr. Thompson asked.

No one dared to be the first to raise his or her hand.

"Uh, Mr. Thompson," Renee Bascom, one of the newest members of the board partially raised her hand, only not to vote, but to ask a question, "due to the sensitivity of this issue, could we submit a written ballot instead?"

Thompson sighed, "I suppose." He had hoped to get this over as swiftly as possible.

Blank pieces of paper were distributed to each school board member. Everyone quickly grabbed a pen and wrote out their vote. Thompson collected the papers and tallied them. It was unanimous.

Brendan Moss returned from his mailbox a mite flustered. The check he had received every two weeks during his administrative leave was now four days late. He'd waited long enough, so he decided to phone the superintendent's office.

"This is Brendan Moss. Is there a reason why my check is delayed?"

"I will connect you with the superintendent.

"Good morning, Mr. Moss." Bailey Thompson's manner seemed contrived, almost like he had been expecting the call. "What can I do for you?"

Moss was perplexed. Perhaps Thompson was not aware that this check was late.

"My check hasn't arrived yet," Brendan announced, growing more and more suspicious, "but you already know that, don't you?"

Thompson was impressed by Mr. Moss' intuition. "Due to our poor financial standing, some payments have been delayed. Your check was sent out today, Mr. Moss. There is no need to worry about the money, but you should not expect to receive many more checks in the future."

"Excuse me?"

"We are in the process of revoking your tenure, Mr. Moss." Thompson droned on. "Once that is official, you will no longer be eligible for compensation during your administrative leave."

"Is the union aware of this?"

"Yes Mr. Moss, the teachers' union has been informed of my decision to suspend your pay, and I imagine that they are preparing a defense on your behalf."

"How come I wasn't notified?"

Mr. Thompson sighed, "I cannot answer that. I suppose that's a question you'll have to take up with your union rep."

Brendan hung up the phone.

Dan Ross was just about ready to leave for the day, when the door to his room was roughly pushed open. He was mildly startled to see Maya Gregg. "Who the hell's side are you on?" she screamed at the president of the Riverton Teachers Association. "I just learned, through some reliable sources, that Moss' tenure is being revoked, and that no one contacted him about it."

"We are preparing a defense."

"Why wasn't Brendan told?"

Ross was ready with an answer. "Albany is behind this. I've been in contact with Linda Malachi, president of the state association, and the wheels are turning. Look Ms. Gregg, this issue involves all of us. Albany wants to do away with a teacher's right to tenure. Moss is their test case. This is too big for us. We need to call in the big guys, and Malachi is doing just that. When I know more, I will let everybody know."

Maya Gregg didn't buy it. Something smelled rotten, and she wanted to know what it was. She especially didn't like hearing that Brendan Moss was being referred to as a test case.

"You listen to me," she said, as she placed her hands on Ross' desk and leaned towards him, "Brendan Moss is not a test case. This is not an experiment we're talking about. He's a man, a father, for God's sake. He's a heart-broken widower who needs an income just like the rest of us. Why wasn't he notified?"

"The investigation into the complaints leveled against him is not going in his favor. Moss was seen at Abby Richardson's house, and a neighbor claims that she saw the pair hugging on the porch."

"And what does our school lawyer have to say about that?"

Ross shook his head, "I have not been in contact with the school's attorney."

"What? Do you care about this at all? Why was his salary check was delayed?"

"You'd have to ask the superintendent," he replied softly.

"I'll do that," Maya Gregg responded firmly as she turned to leave the room.

"I've watched you." She stated accusingly. "Every time one of the staff has failed to get the answer they sought from you, they went to Brendan Moss. Mr. Moss led our union well for so many years. You're new at it and I suspect still a bit jealous of Moss. Get over it and get on with why we elected you in the first place. One of our own needs your help and here you sit on your hands and do nothing!"

Maya Gregg left.

Ross leaned back in his chair. The opportunity he had been offered, to lead the science curriculum in Albany, had been too appealing to dismiss. He had a chance to get out of here, climb the ladder, and sit with the big boys of New York State Education.

His cell phone rang. It was Albany. As Dan Ross listened he grinned widely.

"Thank you so much," he ended. He did it! He was going to be the chairman of the New York State Curriculum Department. He was one of the good old boys.

"No," Linda Malachi, screamed into her cell phone, "you listen to me!'

Sitting at his desk, on the receiving end of the call, Robert Haines grimaced. He had been expecting this.

"No teacher in New York State is going to have their tenure revoked! I will be sending a team of lawyers to the Riverton School District to speak to this Bailey Thompson. I have also learned that Mr. Daniel Ross, the president of Riverton's teachers association, has been offered a comfortable position within the State Education department. I find that rather interesting. We will see you in court!"

Robert Haines was already tired of the whole ordeal, and a part of him wished they'd never started it, but they had had to!

Teachers all across the country were caught up in sex scandals or had been caught abusing drugs and alcohol. Others were simply inept. Some were lazy ditto factory dictators, who sat at their desks daily while untaught students completed worksheets.

Tenure protected all of them from getting what they deserved: fired! If New York State had to be the one to start the ball rolling, then so be it and if he, Robert Haines, had to be the one to help set the precedent then he was ready.

His phone rang. "Daddy!" It was his daughter, Annie. "I won't be able to meet you for lunch today."

Haines frowned. "Why not, honey?"

"Well," she explained excitedly, "there's going to be protest today in front of the State Capitol Building, and I was planning on joining in."

"What are they protesting?"

Annie replied enthusiastically, "The State of New York is trying to get rid of some teacher's tenure!"

'Great,' Haines thought to himself, 'just great'.

The evening's game was against Fairview. The basketball season was winding down, and even though Jonathan wasn't playing a lot of minutes, Brendan was managing to get better sleep. There were only four games left and then the playoffs. Jon was maintaining a good attitude, and the team was winning.

Brendan never did talk to the coach about this son's playing time. He knew that he did the right thing. He kept his mouth shut and supported the team.

Fairview had had a poor season, which meant that there was the potential for a blow-out by Ashton. It also meant that his son would most likely see more playing time, and sure enough, Jonathan Moss did play around fifteen minutes. The kid played well. He was the team's third leading scorer with eleven points.

The following morning, Brendan picked up the local newspaper and read, "Jon Moss also added 11 points for the Panthers". It was nice. It felt good. Brendan felt vindicated. He always knew that Jon could play and play well.

Jon's next game was Friday night in Riverton. It was Brendan's first time back in the building since his unceremonious exit. He was nervous about returning, but there was no way he was going to miss his son's game, and after how well Jon had played on Tuesday, Brendan expected that he would be getting some more playing time this evening. Riverton had a strong varsity team, but without Buster McHale, the superior Ashton squad would comfortably handle the opposition.

Walking into the building was like coming home. The few teachers, who were working the game, collecting tickets or patrolling the hallways, eagerly greeted him. It was nice to be missed. It was nice to be appreciated. As he walked towards the gym, parents standing nearby shook his hand, while others actually made their way out of the stands to welcome him back.

On the side where Brendan entered the gym, the Ashton boys warmed up. Brendan stood and watched them complete their lay-up drill. On the far side of the gym, the Riverton players were also practicing their shots. One of the Riverton boys noticed Mr. Moss, left the drill and ran towards him. The entire Riverton boys' varsity basketball team followed suit. There were hugs, high-fives, and words of encouragement. Apparently, nobody believed the rumors.

Bailey Thompson and Tyler Haden sat from the stands and watched, and neither one was very pleased by what he saw. Thompson wanted to quietly push the case through the courts and be done with it. He worried that he chose the wrong man. People loved this guy.

Tyler Haden's regrets were quite different. He wished he'd never been a participant in the plan to begin with. He thought Moss was a fine teacher and a good man.

Brendan jogged across the gym to the bleachers. He sat alone as was his custom, but he was not alone for long. Two of his former students stopped over to visit. One of them used to be the star player for the Riverton squad, while the other probably never scored a basket in his life. It was Buster McHale and Charles Hayes.

"I was going to call you, but my Mom told me to leave you alone. Man," Buster exclaimed, "it's good to see you!"

"We know you're going to beat this thing," Charles added his support. "You're not guilty of anything, and everybody knows it."

"Do you wish you were out there?" Brendan nudged Buster.

"I'll be back next season."

Brendan was glad to hear that. Then he wondered, 'Will I?'

With five minutes left in the second quarter, the Ashton coach tapped Jonathan Moss on his shoulder. He was going into the game. Once again, Jon played well. He made two free throws, and had an assist and a steal.

As the half neared its' end, Jon made a fourteen foot shot as the buzzer sounded. Brendan leaped to his feet. It was awesome! He couldn't have asked for more. He was so happy for his son.

Then his world came crashing down. Brendan didn't actually see it happen, but he knew something was wrong. The Ashton boys were yelling, screaming for their coach to get over to where they were all huddled around their fallen teammate. All of the spectators were on their feet.

Brendan watched as the head coach of Ashton High sprinted over. He heard him yell for someone to call 911. When the coach moved to the side, the people could see the body.

Jonathan Moss lay on the floor.

Chapter 10

A week after burying his soul mate, Brendan Moss had felt compelled to go visit his wife's gravesite. It was a cold morning. There were flurries in the air, and Brendan stood shaking as he stared at the stone.

"I will never understand this, Lord. She's my life! You took away my life, and I don't know why. How do I go on without her?" he sobbed. For two full minutes, he was unable to speak. His throat filled with phlegm and choked his every breath.

For a brief moment he wondered. Is this how I'm going to die? Will I collapse right here and die of a broken heart?

Dying right there and then was fine with him. That's what he hoped to do. Then he could reunite with his Emily. Then all the pain would be over with.

What about the kids?

"Okay, Lord," he had managed, regaining control over his vocal chords, "I'll get through it, and I will continue for them. Only promise me that nothing will ever happen to them. I cannot go through something like this again."

As Brendan stared at the still, lifeless body of his youngest child, a great fear dominated his spirit. He was angry. Nobody deserved this twice!

Five years ago when he had held his wife's hand, he had prayed feverishly. This time he did not. Why bother? God wasn't going to answer. He didn't last time.

Once they arrived at the hospital, his son was wheeled into the operating room. He was still breathing, but remained unconsciousness. "Please wait out here, Mr. Moss," he was instructed, as they took his son away.

Brendan decided to go for a walk. He hated that hospital. He hated being trapped inside the same building with death.

"'Everything will turn out good for those who love God,'" he started quoting, "Ha! Do you call this good? I've done my part, Lord. I have believed everything You have said in Your Word. I taught my children, and now they won't even go to church with me. Matt argues with me, but I've held fast to my faith. I've trusted You. You took Emily away, yet I persevered. I raised three kids by myself, and they are good kids! I have sacrificed. I have denied myself, and I have done my best. None of it has been easy, but I did it, and this is how You treat me!"

"I'm pissed off!" he yelled out loud, "This shouldn't happen to anyone once, let alone twice! What did I do? He's my son, Lord."

Brendan had an idea. "Years ago, You and I made a great exchange. You took my life, and I got yours. I know it was a one-time deal, but I want to offer you mine again. You take mine and spare Jon's. I don't care how much it hurts or how much I suffer in death. Take me in exchange for him! I'm not kidding, Lord. Your Word says, 'no greater love has a man than this that he lay down his life for another'. I'm laying it down. Do it, Lord. Strike me down. It'll be worth it."

His cell phone rang. It was Tyler Haden. "I was there. How's your son?"

Brendan fell into a fit of tears. He dropped to his knee and tried his best to get the hand that held the phone to stop shaking. He was unable to respond. He hoped Tyler would understand. After a minute, he shut the cell phone, got back to his feet, and walked back towards the hospital. He found Matthew in the parking lot, waiting for him.

"Amanda and Brian are on their way," his older son informed him. His daughter and son-in-law lived a few hours north in the Syracuse area, so it would be a while until they reached Ashton, but it did make him feel a little better knowing that his daughter was coming.

A very long hour and a half later, Brendan and Matthew were summoned to a conference with the medical team in charge of examining Jonathan. They were seated at the end of a wide table by the Chief of Staff, Dr. Terrance O'Toole.

"Let me begin by saying, Mr. Moss, that I believe that we got your son here just in time to save his life."

Brendan's head dropped. "Thank you, Lord, thank you, Lord, thank you, Lord."

The Chief of Staff continued, "Jonathan had a brain aneurism. They are like time bombs, Mr. Moss. You never know when they are going to explode. But in your son's case," Dr. O'Toole actually managed a tiny smile, "although the aneurism was severe, it was not lethal. If the aneurism occurs along a major blood vessel, the chances of survival are slim. Jon's erupted along a minor vessel, so he should be all right." The doctor paused to allow what he said so far to sink in. "We are confident that he will shortly regain consciousness, and when he does, Mr. Moss; it's not going to be pretty."

"What do you mean?" shook Brendan.

"Jonathan is going to experience tremendous head pain. We will of course supply drugs for the pain, but I must be frank with you. Mr. Moss, these drugs can have negative side effects. My theory is that since your son is so young, his body will able to effectively deal with the chemicals, and any damaging side effects will be minimal."

"How long before he can come home?"

Dr. O'Toole sighed, "It could be weeks, Mr. Moss, or," he added, "months. We really don't know. Your son will live. What his life will be like, I won't be able say."

He will live! For now that was good enough.

"You said we got Jon to the hospital just in time, and you referred to major and minor blood vessels. What did you mean by that?"

"Brain aneurisms are tricky," the doctor willingly explained. "There is definitely a time factor. The sooner we can diagnose it, and relieve the pressure on the brain, the better chance the patient has of recovering. Obviously, the smaller and the less vital the sizes of the vessel, the stronger are the odds of survival. Studies are showing that people can be born with a predisposition for an aneurism."

"Are they hereditary?"

"No one really knows, Mr. Moss," Dr. O'Toole quickly replied. "I've never heard of any research into heredity and brain aneurisms. I went through your son's family history and did see that his mother was admitted here five years ago and died of the same thing. I'm sorry. So it is interesting that Jonathan has suffered a similar fate. Except that," the doctor quickly stressed, "your boy will live."

"My wife, Emily, she died of a brain aneurism a couple years back."

"Like I said, I know. Perhaps there is a link between the two."

"Hey Dad," Matt broke in, "I'm going to go downstairs and get a drink. Do you want to come?"

"Yeah. Sure. Why not?"

He and Matt purchased some Cokes from the snack bar, found a table, and sat down silently. Even in happy times Matt wasn't very talkative, so Brendan knew that he would have to be the one to snap the silence. "Do you believe this?"

Matt dropped his head slightly, "It's like Mom all over again. Where is your God in all of this?"

It wasn't really a question. It was a statement. Perhaps he meant it like it sounded. Your God is a phony, because now when you really need him, he's nowhere to be found, and that did make Brendan wonder. Every morning he said his prayers, and one of the things he prayed daily was for the Lord to protect the health and well being of his three children. So why is his son in the hospital?

Or maybe Matt was actually saying something different. Maybe he meant, 'Dad, where is God? We need him right now. Why isn't he answering?'

"I don't know, Matt," he answered honestly. "The Bible claims that good comes to those who believe and trust in him, but to tell you the truth, I don't really see the good in any of this."

"Me neither."

Then it hit Brendan Moss. Matt wanted to talk about God. His agnostic son didn't like what he sees and he wants answers. Talking about God to Matt is something good!

"I have faith," Brendan began, "that your brother is going to be fine. We're all going to be fine, Matt." He stopped to gather his thoughts. "Every morning God hears me. I know he does, and each morning I ask him to protect my children. Now I have no clue just how prayer actually works. I speak to God from my heart and He listens. Somehow there is a power in this process. I make lots of requests. Sometimes God says no, but no matter how, or when, or even if he answers, I trust that He always has my best interests in mind."

"Dad," Matt interrupted, "I'm not looking for a lecture on theology. But maybe we should pray for Jon."

Yeah, that's a good idea. Why don't I just shut up, and we'll pray!

The following morning, his daughter and son-in-law arrived at the house. Brendan took everybody out to Friendly's for breakfast, and then they all headed to the hospital to check up on Jon. Dr. O'Toole was summoned as soon as they arrived.

"We'd like to transfer Jon to Strong Memorial in Rochester. They are better equipped to monitor and evaluate his progress."

"How soon?" Brendan asked.

"I think we should get him up there today. I will make arrangements to have him on a mercy-flight as soon as possible."

This recommendation posed a bit of a financial dilemma for Brendan Moss. If Jon were moved, he would be forced to either rent a place in Rochester or stay indefinitely at a motel, but if that was what Jon needed, that is what would need to be done.

Jonathan still had not regained consciousness, before he was flown to Rochester by helicopter. Brendan promised his non-responsive son that he would join him soon. First there were clothes to wash, bags to pack, and accommodations to be arranged. Brendan phoned Motel 6 in Rochester and made reservations. He felt bad about leaving so soon after Amanda's arrival, but what else could he do?

Life is so, so fast. She was already twenty-four, and since she looked just like her mother, Brendan couldn't help but smile every time he saw her. Back when it was just the three of them, Brendan used to rush home from work to see his two girls. He loved those days.

Brendan put in hours playing his role as a shopkeeper, selling plastic food and toiletries to his daughter. He and Emily sat and watched her sing, dance, and act, and of course, there was always Barbie and Ken. Where did the time go?

Right before he left, Amanda and Brian told him the good news. "Brian and I are expecting," Amanda announced. "I'm due by early September."

Wow! Now that was good to hear! He'd lost his job and his son was in a hospital bed recovering from a brain aneurism, but he was about to become a grandfather!

He dropped his stuff off at the Motel 6 in Rochester, and then hurried over to the hospital to see his son. In Jon's room he made one of the most unexpected, incredible discoveries of his life.

"Hi, Dad!"

Jonathan Moss was awake.

Chapter 11

"We will need to keep him here under observation for a few months," he was informed by Dr. Raul Patel. What he had heard about the doctor had been good, so Brendan decided to simply obey Dr. Patel and do whatever he suggested. Physical therapy appeared to be helping. Jon's speech was becoming more normal and his gait improved daily. The doctors were optimistic, and Brendan's confidence was growing as he watched his youngest on the road to recovery.

Everything was going well, except for his finances. The medical charges were steep, even with his insurance. On top of the hospital bills and fees for physical therapy, there was a motel room and daily restraint food to pay for.

So Brendan took out a loan. The bank cleared the amount that he requested without hesitancy. Since the monthly payments for the loan were steep and beyond his means, a group of ten Riverton teachers got together to financially share the burden. It was all very touching, but it was still not enough.

Jon was recovering, though. That was all that truly mattered. "It's a miracle, Dad," Matthew Moss exclaimed one day.

Brendan had to smile, "I thought you don't believe in miracles?"

Now it was Matthew's turn to smile.

"I've seen a lot of stuff lately. Do you go to a church while you're up here?"

Brendan was stunned. "I found an Assembly of God church in a town called Victor," Brendan shared excitedly, "I don't go every Sunday, but I do plan on going tomorrow."

"Okay, maybe I'll meet you for church in the morning."

Brendan gave his son directions to the church and hugged him good-bye. 'How amazing,' he thought, 'Jon suffers a brain aneurism just like his mother, and yet recovers. His injury also makes an impact on his brother's spiritual life. It raises a question: What's more important, the physical or the eternal?

As his son continued to improve physically, Brendan also noticed that Jon was becoming a bit more 'snippy' about his father's seemingly constant presence at the hospital. That also was a good sign.

"You don't need to be here every day, Dad." Jonathan Moss complained more than once. "I'm in good hands here."

"I'm just here if you need me." Brendan would explain in defense of his concern.

"I'm not a baby anymore." His son replied back.

How true that comment was! Brendan didn't have any more babies to take care of.

"Okay, I'll see you tomorrow."

Brendan had just returned to his motel room and turned on the television, when someone knocked on his door. Brendan got up to answer and found the motel manager in the hallway.

"Uh, listen Mr. Moss," he stammered uncomfortably, "I know you are in the middle of a tough situation with your son right now, but you are way behind on your payments, and corporate has informed us that we need to see some effort on your part to pay the bill."

That was fair enough. "How much do I owe?"

The manager of the Motel 6 hesitated before answering, "It's around three thousand dollars."

"The winner takes home three thousand dollars!" Buster McHale shared as he showed the poster to Charles Hayes.

The two boys were sitting together in the cafeteria during lunch. "How long is the race?" Charles asked.

"It's a half-marathon." Buster replied. "That's thirteen miles." He softened his tone, "You can do this, Charles. You're a fantastic runner. You've got great endurance, and besides, Mr. Moss needs the money."

Charles sighed and resigned, "Okay, I'll do it."

"It's not going well."

Tyler Haden's assessment was not what Bailey Thompson wanted to hear. He urged Haden to elaborate.

"His son is recovering just fine, but Moss is struggling and his financial hardships only make us look bad. The auction to raise money for his son's treatments was the largest fund raiser Riverton has ever put on. I have never seen so many people give in my life."

"You were there?" Thompson asked, astonished.

"He's my friend," Tyler defended himself. "His son could have died. Come on, Bailey, sometimes we need to separate business and friendship. He needs money to pay for all of this, and I'm going to reach deep in my pockets to lend a hand. That's what community auctions are for. I grew up here, and Moss used to be an employee here, not to mention a damn fine teacher if you ask me. I wanted to help out."

"Anything else you want to tell me?"

"Well," Tyler Haden smirked, "the community of Ashton, where Moss and his boys live, is providing the funding for one of our ninth graders to run in a half-marathon up in Buffalo."

"When is this?"

"It's the first week in May." Haden eagerly explained. "First prize is three thousand dollars." He stopped to gather his thoughts. "Charles Hayes, a nice boy and a member of Riverton's track team, is training for the race. Ashton sports boosters are providing coaching, nutritional counseling, running shoes, and attire. They are also providing motel accommodations and supplying food for both him and his coaches while they are in Buffalo."

Thompson grumbled, "And just who is this boy?"

"Charles Hayes."

"And you're planning on going to Buffalo to cheer him on?"

Tyler Haden smiled, "You bet I am. I wouldn't miss this for the world."

Rae Langston was helping her husband pack his things. Pastor Ronald was driving up to Buffalo to spend the night in preparation for the half-marathon tomorrow. Accommodations had made for both Pastor Langston and his wife, but Rae Langston wasn't going.

"Have you at least considered it?"

Rae wouldn't look at him as she answered, "I can't do it."

Pastor Ronald dropped the pants he was folding onto the bed. He walked over to his dear wife, the wonderful woman that he loved, and circled his arms around her waist. Rae leaned back into her husband and sighed.

"I wish I could be more like you," she whispered. "I wish I could somehow find the courage to forgive that young man." Rae loosed herself from her husband's embraced and turned to face him. "I'm not wired like you. Every time I see that boy come into our church, our church, Ronald, I want to run and hide. I want so badly to forgive him, only," she widened her eyes, "I want to forgive him because that's what I'm supposed to do, and I know I just can't.

"Everybody's talking about him like he's some kind of hero. People are saying his message at the Revival Meeting was one of the best they'd ever heard. Kids came out of their seats to accept the Lord. It's an incredible story that should inspire all of us. But I'm not inspired. I hate him, Ronald. I pray that he someday rots in Hell! I want Jesus to say to the Father, 'not this one. I will not exchange my righteousness for his sins'.

"Sometimes I even hate you. I hate that you went to his house to save him. I hate the way you've adopted him like he's your own son. He's not! Your son is dead, and that boy killed him! I hate that people in the church admire him. I cannot see what they see. I still see a bully. I see a grotesque young man who beat up my beautiful only child.

"Every time I go in there," she said, referring to Myles' room, "I start to clean. All I can picture is his blood everywhere, and so I bring in the mop and lots of rags, and I scrub everything. Of course the room was spotless before I went in. I miss him so much! Do you even remember what we have lost?"

It was a brisk May morning.

"Perfect!" Charles Hayes' declared the weather. He stretched his stick-like legs and loosened up. Buster stood beside him at Charles' disposal. Whatever Charles needed or wanted, Buster was ready to go get it. Whether it was a back to lean against or a hand to help stabilize his frame, Buster readily complied.

A loudspeaker reminded the crowd that the race would begin in ten minutes. As Charles walked over to the starting line, Buster ran up and grabbed his shoulders. "Listen man; don't feel like you have to win this race to prove something to any of us. I'm going to be here for you no matter what. I mean that. I know what this is like. I've experienced the pressure and the expectations, and there were times, like in the sectional finals, where I was a bundle of nerves. Hey, you know what, never mind. Just be yourself, relax, enjoy running like you always do, and no matter what happens or where you finish, or if you even finish; I'll be there at the finish line waiting for my pal."

Charles Hayes' eyes sparkled, "I'm going to win this race."

The bold comment was so typical of Charles. It was neither bravado nor conceit; it was just Charles believing in himself and standing firmly on his self-worth.

"Do you know, "Buster replied with a chuckle, "that I love that about you? You never let anybody put you down." Buster moved forward and lifted his little buddy right off the ground in a hug. "Go get 'em."

"I don't have to go get 'em," he bragged. "They're going to have to get me."

As soon as the gun went off, Charles Hayes could sense that this was going to be the best run of his life. His body moved fluidly, his every stride was unlabored, as though a portion of him was floating.

Runners were on all sides of him, but as an experienced competitor, Charles was easily able to separate himself from a mass. This may have been the largest crowd of runners he'd ever been surrounded by, but he knew that an opportunity would eventually present itself. At the half-mile marker, Charles saw an opening.

Charles recognized many runners from past competitions where they would have to run five to ten kilometers. In these shorter races, Charles generally finished third or fourth, falling a little behind the quicker runners. He knew that this race was going to be different. To win a thirteen mile race, you needed to have endurance, stamina, and most importantly, will power. The outcome was going to rely on his ability to overcome pain, and he would have to have the determination to knowingly suffer in order to gain the prize. *Which was what?*

By the three mile mark, Charles knew the answer. His father left his mother, him, and his little sister years ago. Charles loved and admired his Dad, and he thought his father felt the same way about him. In the last three years, he and his Dad had talked on the phone a few times. They always discussed having Charles and his little sister fly out to Arizona, where his Dad lived with his girlfriend, for a visit. It never happened.

In seventh grade, Charles was asked to join a group of eighth graders in a math competition called Challenge 24. Mr. Moss was the advisor. Charles had taken an instant liking to the eighth grade math teacher, who not only encouraged him mathematically, but who had treated him with respect and had taken an interest in Charles' life. Mr. Moss was certainly not the father he missed and needed, but he was an adult male who cared, and Charles looked up to him. Charles never forgot the time Mr. Moss spent with him. It was right that he should try to give something back to Mr. Moss.

At the ten mile mark, Charles could see only three other competitors ahead of him. One was a thirty-something year old man, whom he'd seen at other competitions. Charles remembered that the guy always had a good start, but almost always inevitably faded down the stretch.

By the eleven mile mark, Charles had passed him. Another older man slightly ahead, whom he did not recognize, began breathing heavily. Charles felt fairly confident that he was also pass this man soon. He was not the problem. The real hurdle was catching up to and passing Byron Ehman, who was at least twenty yards ahead.

Charles had gone up against Ehman, who was a senior at nearby Randolph, a few times already, during both the cross-country and track seasons. He had never beaten the skilled runner. He had also never liked him.

With a little more than a mile to go, Charles drew within ten yards of Byron. He kept in mind that the Randolph runner was known for deceiving his competitors. He had heard that Ehman would purposely lag behind at the end of a race, so he could turn it into first gear and blow his opponent away down the stretch.

The older boy was faster and stronger than him. Charles was ok with that. What angered him was the way Byron treated the people he outran. After his victories, the Randolph senior would taunt defeated opponents and grind his body in imitation of his challengers' running styles. Byron Ehman was a bully! Charles' determination grew.

Another bully was in his path. This time there would be no Buster McHale to jump out and rescue him, and Mr. Moss was not going to appear out of nowhere to send Byron Ehman back to class. No, this one was all on him. As Charles pulled even with the Randolph senior, he noted two things. He first noticed Ehman's usual, disdainful sneer that said, "You have no chance to beat me". He next noticed that Byron appeared winded, and so sensed that Ehman's jeer was a façade. His eyes said, 'uh-oh, I've got nothing left'.

Down ahead, Charles could see people waiting at the finish line. He estimated that he had about two hundred more yards to go. He blew past his final adversary and glanced back once. Byron Ehman had no final kick left in him this time. This was not a 5 or 10K race. This was a half-marathon, and this race belonged to him!

There was nothing that stood in his way now. Charles heard someone shouting his name. As he shot his head to the right, he noticed the figure that kept pace beside him and smiled. Buster McHale was running the end of the race right along with him.

Once the race began, Buster freed himself from the crowd and stood off alone. It was chilly and windy, and Buster began to feel more and more depressed. All of the runners were out of sight, and he reverted to the self-deprecating thoughts that pestered him in solitude.

'I don't deserve to live,' he prayed silently. 'I killed a boy, Lord. How can you forgive that? Why would you forgive that? Not only that, but I killed the spirit of his mother. I noticed that she is not here today. Pastor Langston is, but not her. The worse thing about it is that I feel sorrier for myself than I do for the Langstons. I admit it. I do! I hate this guilt.

"I'm here at a race to raise money for Mr. Moss. That's a good thing, isn't it? I did whatever I could to help train Charles. I wanted to help. My intentions were pure. My heart was right. My motives were selfless. So where is the joy that I am supposed to feel?"

Buster's dour mood clung to him like cellophane. He sought eye contact with Pastor Ronald, but Mr. Langston stared dolefully into the mist. Pastor, too, had other things on his mind besides the race.

Pastor Langston thought about Charles Hayes. He had been Myles only friend. He knew that Charles had always made it a point to encourage Myles to overcome his depression, and to trust that there would be a brighter future. His wife had done the same.

Poor Rae. She couldn't forgive, and she couldn't forget her devastating loss, but who would expect her to? It had only been a few months since...

The pastor couldn't even complete his thought. He couldn't exist where the memories of his son were so real, but Rae existed there. Pastor Ronald had to forgive the McHale boy. He forgave him, because the bitterness of un-forgiveness would have destroyed him. He had to do it. Otherwise, it would have killed him.

He glanced over at Buster, but Buster was distracted. Buster was staring in awe. Charles Hayes was coming down the stretch and there were no other challengers in sight! Without a thought, he began sprinting towards his little friend. Charles seemed so focused, that Buster believed he ran to his side without Charles noticing. Buster shouted out Charles' name and began to tear.

"Everything will turn out for the good for those who love God". Charles did it! He had encouraged him, but Buster hadn't really believed he could win. But Charles believed it!

As Charles Hayes crossed the finish line, a winner of $3,000, and owner of his first major victory, he was tackled from behind. Buster McHale had played football his whole life. His reputation was unparalleled in Western New York. When he hit you, you knew it! Buster had probably made thousands of tackles in his young career, but of all the tackles Buster McHale had ever made, this one he enjoyed the most.

The initial impact took Charles' breath away. The victor hit the ground. He was immediately lifted off the grass and held high into the air. Buster McHale held Charles up over his head like he was the Vince Lombardi Trophy or the Stanley Cup. It was the best moment either one of them could ever remember.

Chapter 12

The PBIS meeting was set for 3 o'clock. PBIS, an acronym for Positive Behavior Intervention Services, was the new hot topic in New York Public Schools. Teachers, administrators, and parents had come up with a new plan for combating the rampant disrespect for authority, the lack of initiative, the failing grades, and the widespread apathy that was evident in many school districts, Riverton included. Since disciplining unruly students was becoming more difficult, PBIS was introduced to fight the disintegration of the public schools.

PBIS suggested that instead of handing out punishments to students who exhibited incorrect behavior, teachers and administrators should reward students who did their work, paid attention in class, and addressed adults properly. At Riverton the plan was to hand out coupons. Each coupon was a small piece of paper, signed by the authority figure who gave it to the student. One coupon might buy a piece of candy, fifty would be worth a free homework pass, and one hundred coupons might purchase popcorn and a drink. Coupons were supposed to be easy to obtain. A child who completed his or her work and stayed out of trouble could gain as many as fifteen to twenty coupons in a single day. The philosophy was simple. If the misbehaving boys and girls see that kids are getting stuff for good behavior, than there's an incentive for these boys and girls to do the right thing and get in on the good stuff as well.

At 3 o'clock in Albany, Governor Raleigh McDevitt had just finished his impromptu speech on the status of public education in New York. He willingly accepted the reporters' invitation to answer some questions. A man in the front row asked, "Do you think your proposal to eliminate a teacher's right to tenure will pass in the State Legislature?"

McDevitt cleared his throat, "I am very confident that tougher teacher evaluations will be constructed which will serve as a national model for identifying the best teachers and for firing the worst. For the time being, I have set a deadline for a state-wide template to be produced."

In the Riverton Middle School Library the leaders of the PBIS meeting were waiting to begin. The five teachers seated around the long table were waiting for three more coaches to arrive. "So what exactly happened in the seventh grade wing after lunch today?" the Home and Careers teacher posed to no one in particular. "You're on the code yellow team, Gary; what happened?"

"Some kid on drugs flipped out," Gary Schubert, a seventh grade English teacher, casually explained. "He had a pair of scissors in one hand and a lacrosse stick in the other. Even when the police showed up, the kid was still defiant. He told the cops, 'I'm taking somebody down with me'. Can you believe a thirteen year old would say that to the police? The kid was all drugged up. Finally though, he surrendered."

"Have you received a response from the State United Teachers Union?" a tall, older man boldly asked.

McDevitt did not hesitate in his answer. "The union has claimed that forces beyond a teacher's control, such as a parent losing their job, a family divorce, or a student dealing with depression can harm a classes' performance and affect a teacher's evaluation. They argue that a poor evaluation should then not be used as a cause for dismissal."

The same reporter interrupted, "Well, Governor McDevitt, that is a valid criticism. Is it not?"

"How about Teddy Swanson?"

"What did you hear?" another member of the PBIS team wondered aloud.

"Supposedly, his mother found him in his bedroom hanging by a rope," the girls' basketball coach shared. "They rushed him to the psyche ward, and I heard he's okay."

"Luke Banner did the same thing less than two days later," Gary Schubert interjected. "It is like Myles Langston's suicide was the start of an epidemic. Why don't these kids enjoy their lives?"

"I don't agree," answered McDevitt, "Our children are our top priority. Regardless of what is going on in their lives at home, our teachers should be providing a safe and stimulating environment for our young people. If teachers and administrators can create an atmosphere of safety where learning can take place, then whatever baggage a child is carrying can be dealt with. New York State students should be thriving in our schools, not failing and dropping out. A solid, well-applied teacher evaluation system should solve the majority of our problems."

"He threw a punch at Mr. Johnson?"

"No, he didn't actually throw the punch," Mr. Schubert shared. "Bryce did raise his hand and shake his fist at Mr. Johnson though."

"So what happened after that?"

Gary Schubert sighed, "Johnson took him down to the office and explained to Mr. Haden what happened. From what I've heard, Tyler let the kid off and sent him back to class."

"There was no in-school or out of school suspension?"

"No," Schubert grinned, "he went back to class as though nothing ever happened."

"Why?"

Mr. Schubert leaned back in his chair and grimaced, "Haden said, that Bryce said Mr. Johnson provoked him."

"Provoked him how?"

Once again Schubert made a face, "He refused to let the kid put his head down on his desk and made him do his work."

The girls' basketball coach couldn't suppress a smile, "What a lousy guy!"

"How much will standardized testing play into these new evaluations?"

"At least twenty percent of a teacher's evaluation will be directly correlated to state test scores. This percentage could vary and be as high as forty percent of the evaluation. It will depend on negotiations between school districts and their unions."

A young reporter, who was attending his very first address by the Governor of New York, raised his hand. McDevitt acknowledged the younger man, anticipating a benign question.

"Governor McDevitt, with all due respect, are you kidding? All I'm hearing is how the teachers are the problem and that if the state implements some ingenious evaluation system, than everything will turn out all right. Seriously? I'm only five years out of high school, so I can tell you; the teachers are not the problem. At my high school in Binghamton, uninvolved parents were a huge issue. Many of my classmates came from homes where alcoholism, drug abuse, and violent outbursts were common, and their lifestyles did affect their performance. Do you really think that if the English teacher meets the evaluation criteria, that now little Johnny is going to learn?" The kid paused. "Why are you blaming the messenger?"

Chapter 13

Brendan Moss hung up the phone. Maya Gregg had called to tell Brendan that there was going to be a special Board of Education Meeting tomorrow night at seven o'clock, and the meeting concerned him!

The Board meeting was being held in the auditorium. School Board Meetings were generally open to the public, but the announcement of this particular gathering was purposely kept quiet. "Let's just get this over with," began Bailey Thompson. "I know that none of us want to do what we have to do, but the decision that we make today will benefit the education of our children..."

Both back doors of the auditorium crashed open. The bright lights from the hall illuminated the dim room. The men and women seated at the table in front of the stage shielded their eyes. People walked through the doors and headed their way. Lots of people!

Leading the parade on one side was Maya Gregg. On the other side was Linda Malachi. Maya Gregg and Linda Malachi walked up to the front row, and from both sides motioned for those who had followed to be seated.

Teachers, custodians, guidance counselors, bus drivers, and over a hundred parents packed in the auditorium. The rows filled quietly and quickly. "Hello, Robert," Mrs. Malachi greeted the thoroughly embarrassed

Commissioner of Education. "Let me begin by saying that no one is going to have their tenure revoked tonight."

Before she could continue, another person entered the auditorium. Brendan Moss had attended several of the Board of Education meetings in the past, but he'd never seen such a large crowd. This was going to be interesting!

Maya Gregg motioned for Moss to sit beside her. She looked at Linda Malachi and mouthed, "This is Brendan Moss". Malachi smiled to show that she understood and then resumed her speech.

"Ladies and gentlemen, the New York State Department of Education is attempting to use Mr. Moss in a case to set a legal precedent. He," she pointed at Brendan, "is their scapegoat."

"That is not true," Robert Haines muttered.

"Mr. Haines," she nodded in the direction where the Commissioner of Education sat, "is hoping to eliminate tenure. He is hoping to give school districts the power to terminate the employment of any teacher, and he plans to do this by taking away the tenure of one man. By setting a precedent in the courts, teachers will legally be laid off throughout the state." Malachi dropped her arms to her side, "Let me be honest with you. It is true that tenure has protected some men and women who should not be teachers. We've all been in school, and I am sure that we have all had a teacher we were disappointed by. Maybe they were lazy, perhaps they didn't even like kids, but he or she was guaranteed the job because of tenure. That's the reality. Nevertheless, I believe that the continuation of the institution of tenure to our educational system is crucial!

"The world we older folks grew up in doesn't exist anymore. There was a time when students and parents alike held teachers in high regard. When my parents ran into one of my teachers in town, they listened intently and valued every word that man or woman had to say about me. My, my, my," Malachi shook her head derisively, "how things have changed!

"Please understand. The vast majority of our students are here to learn. They really are. Most parents are still thrilled to hear what the teacher has to say about their child. They do teach their children right from wrong, and they do hold their kids to high standards and expectations.

"But not all of today's parents and students are on board! There is a small, and I mean small, portion of parents who do not see teachers as the past generations once did. They put on blinders. They pretend that it is not their child who disrupts and interferes with the learning process. Unfortunately, it is these poorly behaved children who give the entire educational system the black eye we currently display. Our image as an institution has been tarnished and we are perplexed. We wonder, 'What are we to do'"?

Just then the back doors of the auditorium were torn open once again. This time, the intruders were much younger. Charles Hayes led a group of fifty high school and middle school students down the right side aisle, while Buster McHale did the same down the left. The kids took seats, right behind the adults who had preceded them.

"We're sorry to rudely interrupt," Buster stated sincerely, "but we just found out about this, and well," he spread out his muscular arms, "we all love Mr. Moss, so we came to show our support."

Robert Haines' mind repeated as single phrase. The same supposition dominated the thoughts of superintendent, Bailey Thompson. 'We chose the wrong man; we chose the wrong man; we chose the wrong man'.

Linda Malachi welcomed the newest guests and continued her speech, "At some point the teachers became the enemy. I believe I know why. A child is a mirror of his or her parents, and when a teacher holds up this mirror to a negligent parent, they do not like what they see! The looking glass shows that they are self-centered, poorly behaved, and selfish! Most of us are parents. I'm not ashamed to admit that my very own children have let me down, embarrassed me, and made me look bad on occasion, but I have never blamed anyone but myself and my children for our shortcomings."

Incredibly, but hardly a surprise any longer, one of the back doors leading into the auditorium was opened again. Three young people, three males and one female, came down the aisle to join the others. Amanda, Moss' daughter, and her husband Brian, walked with Moss' two sons. Jonathan Moss moved unimpeded. Brendan shot to his feet and moved to greet his family. Enthusiastic chatter spread throughout the crowd. Buster McHale threw his arms up in the air, as if he had just scored a touchdown.

"These parents," resumed Linda Malachi, "would love the power to take the mirror away. Administrators have already bowed down and allowed them to berate their child's teachers. Revoking tenure would give these same parents the power to have these teachers fired from their jobs. We cannot let that happen. Parents, who don't even know how to control a teenager, have no right to decide who is fit to teach.

"If we, and now I'm referring to our entire public school system, allow a teacher's right to tenure to be abolished tonight; the security of education will crumble along with it. Any troublemaking parent in a snit will have us in court forever! Tenure is hardly a perfect system, and it's probably not a good way to run a business, but that's just the point. Teaching is not a business.

"I taught school for over twenty-five years. I didn't choose this profession for the money or the recognition. I became a teacher, because I love young people. Now let's face it, young people have changed, and in many cases their attitudes and behaviors are getting worse, but," she held up her hand, "I still love them!"

"These kids need us, and they need teachers like Mr. Moss. Is he hard on them at times? You bet he is! That's because he cares.

"Teachers don't just see these students as they are. We see an unpolished jewel, because we are blessed with the ability to envision a refined, finished product. Once you visualize what a kid can be, you work to help it happen. Good teachers prune their students. Does it hurt? Will these wild roots respond in resentment? Yes, sometimes they will. Should we change our loving, caring approach because they went home crying to Mommy and Daddy? Do we back down from teaching responsibility, when Mom and Dad did not?

"Our right to tenure is the core of our strength. It protects us when we are unduly attacked. Tenure is the teacher's anchor in an unsteady educational system that has already been weakened by its inconsistency. Tenure says to both children and parents: We are here for the long haul. If anyone votes to remove tenure, then they are voting to remove the foundation of our entire educational system. So," she challenged the Riverton Board of Education, "if you want to see the school system collapse, than revoke Mr. Moss' tenure."

The people in the auditorium sat quietly, until a young boy stood up near the back and made his way down to the front of the auditorium, excusing himself as he moved past his seated peers. "My name is Oscar Campenelli," he began, "and I am one of the reasons why we are all here tonight."

Brendan Moss and Maya Gregg exchanged glances. Their eyes spoke the same words: 'Are you kidding me?'

"Mr. Moss was charged with injuring a student," Oscar continued without a trace of nerves. "I'm that student. I started a fight, and I broke a boy's nose. I would have done more damage if Mr. Moss had not interfered." Oscar took a deep breath, "He may not remember this, but one day after I started a fight in the cafeteria, he pulled me aside and told me something I never forgot.

" I thought he was going to yell at me like he usually does," Oscar giggled. "A lot of kids were afraid of him, but I never was. When he got mad and tough with me, I would just fold my arms across my chest and smile. That's because I thought I was cool. Mr. Moss knew I wasn't. So after the cafeteria fight, he pulls me into the hall, looks me right in the eye, and instead of yelling at me, he tells me this, 'You don't fool me, Campenelli. You might fool everyone else around here, but I've got some special insight."

Brendan's eyes widened. He too remembered. 'Maybe these kids do listen to me!' he thought.

"Mr. Moss said, 'I know what you've got inside of you'," Brendan mouthed the words as Oscar said them aloud, "and it's good, and it's clean, and it's right. I cannot wait to see what a success you become'. Nobody ever said anything like that to me before. No one ever cared about how I hurt, who I was, or what would become of me, until Mr. Moss. And I now bet Mr. Moss isn't the only teacher who feels this way.

"Well anyway, when he broke up the fight between Billy and me, I tried a trick that my older brother taught me. When Mr. Moss pulled me away, I made myself fall so that it would look like he threw me to the ground. I took my fingernail and dug into my own face to draw blood. My brother told me that he did that once with a teacher, and the guy got in big trouble, so I figured I'd try it too.

"You guys," he pointed his finger towards a group of middle school teachers who were seated together, "probably have no idea how important you are. We need you so badly. I know kids like me act like we have no respect for you, but I think a lot of us are just jealous. We're jealous of your happiness and of your accomplishments, and we are especially jealous of how we see you parent your own children, because we know what a lousy job our parents did. You guys come to work every day with a good attitude.

It's like you're expecting us to listen, even when we didn't the day before. You care about us.

" I know that I can speak intelligently. I didn't fail tests, because I was incapable." He pointed at Mr. Moss. "He knew that. I was a failure because I didn't try. No one and nobody will reach a kid who doesn't want to learn. Period! Pour on the counseling, and give us the damn answers if you like. Nothing is going to work until we care about our teachers and care about ourselves."

The collective applause startled the young orator. Brendan Moss noticed something. Oscar was a nice-looking boy. Minus the scowl and his usual unkempt appearance, the kid was actually strikingly handsome.

"Mr. Moss," Oscar called out loudly, "thank you for everything. You helped change my life, and though I can never repay you, I promise you that I will go on and be the man you alone saw on the inside of me."

Oscar Campenelli, former punk, former young alcoholic, former drug dealer, and former loser, walked back to his seat to a standing ovation. As he shuffled his way past other students towards his seat, he was further encouraged by pats on the back and even a couple of hugs. One hug came from a young boy who grabbed Oscar from behind. It was Billy Weston.

Soon after Oscar was seated, another young person strode up to the front of the auditorium. This time it was a young girl. She was petite with dark brown hair and tattoos covered her arms, legs, and upper chest.

"I'm Abby Richardson," she began, "and I'm very uncomfortable speaking in front of all of you, but for Mr. Moss, I will do it.

"When I had my baby, I was all alone. My parents deserted me, and even my Aunt was disgusted with me. I was pregnant, so to be perfectly honest with you, I really didn't care how I did on my state exams. I had bigger issues to deal with.

"When I started having contractions, I was in a panic. I didn't even have a ride to the hospital. I thought of Mr. Moss, because, well," she shrugged, "he's Mr. Moss!"

Maya Gregg draped her arm around Brendan's shoulder. What a salute that was! A young girl reaches out to you for the simplest of reasons, because you are who you are!

"Mr. Moss agreed immediately. He drove a half-hour to come get me, and then drove another half-hour with me to the hospital. He stayed, and even held my baby.

"Weeks later he went out shopping and bought both of us Christmas gifts. For this he gets in trouble? It broke my heart to hear the dirty rumors about him having a sexual relationship with me. I just wanted to say that nothing inappropriate ever went on between me and Mr. Moss. He was my teacher; I liked him and I knew I could call on him during my time of need." Abby stopped and dropped her eyes to the floor. "Thank you. That's really all I have to say."

Linda Malachi rose again to face the audience. "Are you ready to take your vote?" She challenged the members of the Riverton Board of Education.

Superintendent Bailey Thompson stood to pass out the paper ballots he had prepared in advance.

"No," Linda Malachi pronounced, "we want to see the hands."

Thompson asked, "All those in favor of revoking the tenure of Mr. Brendan Moss, please raise your hand."

No one.

"All those opposed?"

Every hand at the table shot up.

Tyler Haden couldn't help himself. The Principal of Riverton Middle School leaned back his head and hooted. Maya Gregg wrapped her arms around the guy seated on her other side and kissed him on the cheek.

Buster McHale got to his feet and danced down the aisle. He threw open the door to the hallway and was about to mimic the howl of the principal when he found Pastor and Mrs. Langston blocking his way.

"We'd like to talk." Pastor asked.

"So would I," Buster said to Rae.

Brendan Moss stood up slowly. It was nice to be reinstated, nice to hear the accolades from former students, and nice to see the incredible support of his colleagues and the community of Riverton, but the best thing of all was walking out with this son Jon under his arms. One thing he knew without a doubt: *It's great to be a school teacher!*

Brendan Moss got up early and left the house by 6:20. He arrived at the Riverton Middle School parking lot by 6:50. He gathered his materials and entered the building. Inside the same room he'd taught in for the past twenty-five years, Brendan placed his books on his old desk and turned on his computer. He had a novel to finish.

By seven-thirty kids were at their lockers and other teachers began standing outside their rooms to supervise the hallways. Brendan had an odd feeling that he'd never left.

"You ready?" Maya Gregg called to him from across the hall. Brendan raised his thumb.

A minute before homeroom announcements were due to begin, he was approached by Tyler Haden. Once all of the kids had filtered into their homerooms, he stood alone in the hall with the middle school principal.

"I have so much to apologize for," Tyler started, making sure that no one could hear, "but I want you to know how glad I am to have you back, and even though there's only two weeks left in the school year, I expect as always, that you will do a good job."

Brendan trusted Haden's sincerity. "Thanks, Tyler." They shook hands.

The morning classes went smoothly. Brendan could tell that a majority of the students were also glad to have him back. For lunch he decided to join a group of teachers and aides in the faculty room.

Following some small talk, a gentleman who worked in the guidance department asked Brendan, "What do you think about running for union president next fall?"

"Doesn't Dan Ross still have a year left?" Brendan replied.

"Ross resigned his post," a teacher's aide informed him. "Supposedly, he was in line for some big-wheel position with State Ed, and once that fell through he got mad and quit the union. Ask Maya. She knows all about it."

Right after lunch Brendan had what he remembered as his most difficult class. There were five or six kids who required extra assistance, and as usual, Mrs. Swick, a teacher's aide, was assigned to be in the room with Brendan to keep the challenging students on task while he taught.

When Brendan gave the kids a warm-up sheet of math problems, one student put his head down.

"Get your head up!" Moss demanded.

Mrs. Swick came over and tapped the boy's shoulder.

"Can I go to the nurse?" the kid asked. "I need my meds."

"Sure," Brendan readily permitted, "you can go to the nurse as soon as you complete the warm-up sheet."

"I need to go now," the disgruntled youth complained.

"First do the work."

"My meds are for my anger issues and I'm starting to get angry now."

Moss did not back down. "Is that comment supposed to scare me?"

"I'm getting mad enough to whip your ass!" he called and stormed out of the room.

Mrs. Swick looked over at Mr. Moss and smiled, "It's good to be back, isn't it?"

Brendan took her sarcastic comment more seriously than she intended it. He too smiled. "It sure is!"

Summer vacation was uneventful, with the exception of watching league basketball games in Ashton. Matt and Jon were on two different opposing teams, and Brendan attended each and every game. Yes, Jonathan Moss was back on the court and playing like nothing had ever happened. Dr. O'Toole assured Brendan that a reoccurrence was highly unlikely. God is good!

The following school year began, and Brendan's life was back to being routine, but at the end of September he traveled up to Syracuse to wait for the arrival of his first grandchild. With his daughter in labor, Brendan could only sit downstairs and be patient.

"Mr. Moss?" A receptionist came up to him. "You can see your daughter now."

Brendan hurried to the maternity ward. It was a girl! She had dark hair and blue eyes. She was beautiful.

"Her name is Emily," Amanda told her dad.

"I like that name," answered Brendan, as he gazed at his new grandchild.

'This has been a pretty good life,' he thought to himself, 'and it's not over yet!'